FORSAKEN

Also by Vanessa Miller

Former Rain

Abundant Rain

Latter Rain

Rain Storm

Through The Storm

FORSAKEN

VANESSA MILLER

www.urbanchristianonline.net

Urban Books
1199 Straight Path
West Babylon, NY 11704

ISBN- 13: 978-1-60162-934-0
ISBN- 10: 1-60162-934-6

First Printing October 2009
Printed in the United States of America

10   9   8   7   6   5   4   3   2   1

*This is a work of fiction. Any references or similarities to actual
events, real people, living, or dead, or to real locales are intended
to give the novel a sense of reality. Any similarity in other names,
characters, places, and incidents is entirely coincidental.*

Distributed by Kensington Corp.
Submit Wholesale Orders to:
Kensington Publishing Corp.
C/O Penguin Group (USA) Inc.
Attention: Order Processing
405 Murray Hill Parkway
East Rutherford, NJ 07073-2316
Phone: 1-800-526-0275
Fax: 1-800-227-9604

This book is dedicated to my nephew, Eric Leon Epps, Jr.
May you always know the love of family and the God
who forgives us all.

Acknowledgments

Anyone who reads my books knows that I write restoration stories. In order to write about restoration, I have to deal with sinful characters. However, this is the first book in which I dared to have a fallen pastor as my main character. As I prayed about writing *Forsaken*, I became convinced that this was the restoration message God wanted to get out to His people. I began to test the waters at book club meetings, telling everyone who would listen about a wayward pastor's path back to God. Each member of the book clubs I told JT Thomas's story to encouraged me to hurry up and finish the book. So, I would like to thank all the book club members who took the time to listen and offer their input into JT's struggle to make amends for all his wrongdoing.

A special thanks also goes out to my agent, Natasha Kern. I appreciate all the time you spend on my projects, and thanks for getting *Forsaken* sold! I would also like to thank my editor at Urban Christian, Joylynn Jossel. As always, your edits help me to rethink certain aspects of the novel and make it a better product all together; you're the best. The graphic artist at Urban Christian does such a great job on my book covers that I have to take a moment to acknowledge that fact. Natalie Weber, at Urban Books, has been a great help to me also. Whenever I have a question or need to get something done, she has always been there for me. Thanks, Natalie, I know that you are very busy, but I wanted you to know that the extra effort you put in hasn't gone unnoticed.

Finally, I cannot forget to acknowledge my family. A special thanks to my daughter Erin and my grandbaby, Amarrea, whose presence brings me so much joy; to my mother, Patricia Harding, for traveling the world with me while I promote my books. I would also like to thank my sister Debra, and cousins Kim and Schilala for believing in me and helping me to accomplish my dreams. At times, this has been a hard journey, but family makes the difference.

PROLOGUE

"**Y**our husband is cheating on both of us." Those happy–home stealing words ricocheted through Cassandra's mind as she drove to Faith Outreach Church to confront her husband, Pastor JT Thomas. She willed herself not to cry; not to think about the five wonderful years of marriage she'd had with JT.

She pulled into the first lady's parking spot, turned off the engine, and put her hand on her swollen stomach. No, she couldn't even think about the child growing inside her. If her life with the magnificent pastor of Faith Outreach Church had been nothing but a lie, and if the woman who had the audacity to telephone her was telling the truth, then JT was going to admit it to her face.

Pressing her hand into the small of her back, she ambled her way through the fellowship hall. The lower the baby dropped, the harder walking became. But Cassandra loved every minute of being pregnant. This was her second pregnancy. Their first child was a girl, but she had died after only a few precious moments on earth. It had been hard to deal with, but she and JT had made it through; now they had other problems.

JT's office was toward the back of the building, right across from the sanctuary. Another ten steps and she would see what the good pastor had to say for himself.

"First Lady, can I get you something?"

Cassandra smiled as she weebled around to greet Deacon Joe Benson, the almost seven foot, solid built man who didn't take down to anybody, but still managed to treat her gently. "No. I'm okay."

"Well, just let me know if you need anything," he told her.

I need a faithful husband, Cassandra thought, and wanted to beg Deacon Benson to go get that for her. But it wasn't Deacon Benson's fault that JT was one way behind the pulpit and quite another at home. So she patted him on the shoulder and said, "I will, Deacon Benson, thank you."

She opened the door to JT's office without bothering to knock. Pastor Jerome Tyler Thomas was holding court behind his mahogany desk, while Carl Johnson and Deke Smalls poured over the drafts for the reconstruction of the sanctuary with him. JT was being groomed to become the next great televangelist, and the sanctuary was being renovated to accommodate all the equipment that would be needed to bring forth his vision.

She looked down at this muscular built, honey–toned, greenish–grey eyed man that she adored and planted her feet firmly, which was hard for a weeble to do. "I need to talk to you, JT."

JT was focused on the plans before him. He glanced at his watch. "Can't right now, Sanni."

Sanni was JT's pet name for her. She loved the sound of it as it fell from his lips. It made her feel special. Every time he said it she was reminded of that sweet Bible passage that said, "I am His and He is mine." But not today. Today, she was fat, pregnant, and married to a cheater. She stomped her foot. "Will you look at me?"

JT straightened and caught a glimpse of the tears bubbling over the lids of his wife's eyes. Carl grabbed the plans and rolled them up.

"We can review these after this morning's service, Pastor," Deke told him as he and Carl left the room.

Coming around the desk, JT's leg stiffened. He stopped, straightened it out, and continued moving toward Cassandra with that slight limp that was characteristic JT. It was also the bone of another contention between them. JT wouldn't talk to her about the one physical imperfection he had. Whenever she asked about the limp, he would just grunt and say it was nothing. But nothing didn't leave a scar on the upper left thigh. And nothing didn't call her house claiming to be sleeping with her husband.

He hugged Cassandra, and then walked her over to his black leather couch. "Sit down, honey. Is something wrong with the baby? Are you having contractions?"

"No, nothing like that," she told him, sliding into her seat.

Looking at his watch again, he said, "Well, can it wait then? I've got to be in the pulpit in less than five minutes."

When they were first married, JT never allowed anyone in his office five, ten, or even twenty minutes before he had to preach. That was his time with the Lord. JT used to say that he couldn't rightly give direction to his congregation if he hadn't heard from God first. She'd admired and respected him for that. But that was then.

Today, she pulled herself off the couch and sneered at him. "Thought you'd get away with it didn't you? Thought I'd never figure it out?"

He grabbed his Bible from the desk. "I don't know what you're rambling about, Cassandra, but I have to go."

As he opened the door to step out, his wife yelled, "Your woman called me this morning. She says you're cheating on both of us. Is that true, husband?"

JT closed the door, then advanced on his wife. "Why would you say something like that in the house of God?"

At five foot three she was no match for JT's six foot physic, but she stood in his face and challenged him anyhow. "Why would you do something like that in God's house? I mean, come on, JT. The deaconess? Guess we know who she's serving, huh?

"No baby, you've got it wrong. I could never do that to you." He tried to put his hands on her shoulder, but she moved away.

She wiped the tears from her cocoa-cream face, then ran her hand through her bob-length hair. "Not just me, JT. You've done this to God, too."

Turning away from her, JT lowered his head. "I'm not perfect, Sanni, but I do love you. If you believe nothing else, please—"

She shook her head. "No. I'm not listening to a word you have to say, not anymore. You're going to pay for what you've done to me. I'll go out there and let this congregation know what the good pastor is really like."

He grabbed her as his eyes dilated with rage. "Oh, no you won't. Do you hear me? Just shut your mouth and listen."

"Let go of me, JT."

They struggled. She tried desperately to pull away from him. JT inched her backward until he had her against the wall. "I'm not cheating on you, Sanni. All I ever wanted was to be with you. I moved heaven and earth to make that happen."

"Why do you always say that? You postponed the wedding twice, how is that moving heaven and earth?"

"That had nothing to do with how I felt about you. For the love we share."

Cassandra wanted to spit in his face for the heartache his love had brought her. For how he'd trampled on her dreams. But a pain shot through her so fierce, she forgot about JT and his whore mongering. Forgot how he and Bishop Turner had trained her to be a fine first lady, and let out a yelp that caused Deacon Smalls to peak his head into the office.

He looked toward JT. "Sorry to interrupt, Pastor. But the congregation can hear y'all. Just thought you'd want to know."

JT released Cassandra. She grabbed her belly, fell on her knees, and screamed again. "Well, tell one of 'em to call an ambulance instead of pressing their ear against my door. Can't you see that my wife's in labor?" JT yelled.

"Sorry, sir. We'll call the ambulance right away."

As Deacon Smalls ran toward the phone, JT sat on the floor next to his wife. "Are you okay, Sanni?"

"It hurts, JT."

He put her head in his lap. "Tell me what to do, Sanni. I'll do anything to relieve your pain."

Margie Milner rushed into the office, her three-inch pumps crushing down on the plush burgundy carpet. Cassandra pointed at the deaconess in her long dress, as her tears fell into JT's lap. "Get rid of her."

"I'll do whatever you want, Sanni. Just please don't lose our baby."

CHAPTER 1

November, 2009

"Why do you stay?"

Cassandra's mother had asked her the same question for the last three years. Ever since she'd foolishly confided all their secrets. She used to tell her mother that she stayed for love, because her sons needed a father. Because she still remembered the man JT used to be, and would wait forever for him to return.

"Girl, I know you hear me talking to you," her mother said.

Cassandra picked up her purse. "Look, Mama, today is the church's anniversary and the first day of our TV ministry. Let's just go to church and celebrate with everyone else. Okay?" It had taken them two years to raise the money for their television ministry, and then another year to get the time slot JT wanted.

Mattie reached in the closet to get her grandchildren's coats. "You can celebrate with that snake if you want, but

I'm going to sit in the church nursery with Jerome and Aaron."

Cassandra rolled her eyes. She was getting annoyed with her mother. Mattie was normally a wonderful person to be around, but when they discussed matters of the church, she became cantankerous and insulting.

"I know you're not getting upset with me, Cassandra Ann?"

Cassandra laid Aaron, her eight-month-old son, on the couch and put his snow suit on him, while Mattie took Jerome, her three-year-old, and put his jacket on. "Sometimes, I wonder why you even go to church, Mother. I mean, you don't seem to like anybody there."

"I go for comic relief," Mattie told her daughter as she zipped up Jerome's jacket. "Which reminds me; I've got a new joke for you." Rubbing her hands together, she began, "A pastor and an assistant pastor were in church on Sunday morning arguing over who had the most women."

Cassandra raised her hand. "I don't want to hear it."

Mattie ignored her. "The pastor finally told the assistant pastor, 'I know how to resolve this. Every woman who walks through the door that you've been with, you say the word *mark*, and each time a woman I've been with comes through the door, I'll do the same. Then we'll see who has the most marks'.

"The people started arriving to church. One woman walked through the door and the pastor said, 'Mark.' Another woman came through the door, and the assistant pastor said, 'Mark.' Some more women came in and the pastor said, 'Mark, mark.' Then a few more women strolled in, and the assistant pastor said, 'Mark, mark, mark.'

"The pastor looked at him and said, 'Fool, that's my wife and two oldest daughters.' And the assistant pastor said, 'I don't care, I said, *Mark, mark, mark.*' "

The look of horror and astonishment on Cassandra's

face escaped Mattie's attention as she laughed all the way to the car.

As they drove to church, Cassandra wanted to tell her mother that she needed to pray about the things she said concerning men of God. But she couldn't bring herself to chastise her own mother. So she silently prayed that God would have mercy on her mother and lead her in the right path. Then she tried a safer subject. "JT wants you in the sanctuary with us. Can you please do this for me, Mama?"

"Girl, who you kidding? Once that jackleg gets to skinning and grinning in front of that camera, he won't even know if God Himself showed up."

Sometimes Cassandra feared that God would strike her mother down for all her disrespect. She couldn't put it off any longer. "Mama, it's not right to speak about a man of God in such a way."

Mattie Daniels gave her only child a knowing smirk. "What you talking 'bout? I would never open my mouth against a man of God."

JT was in the pulpit gesturing and pontificating, when Cassandra and her mother walked down the aisle and took their front row seats. The pulpit area had been redesigned about six months ago in preparation for the new TV ministry. It had once been cramped and overflowing with choir members. Now the choir sat in the balcony, and wingback chairs lined the side of the pulpit. Only important people were allowed to sit in those wingback chairs. Gone was the acrylic podium she had bought her husband on their first anniversary. It had been replaced by a handcrafted red oak monstrosity.

"As I always say," JT told the congregation, "nothing gets done, unless somebody does it. Just like the Bible says, faith without works is dead."

Cassandra resolved to sit through yet another of JT's

self-empowerment messages. But still she found herself wondering where God fit in all his "nothing gets done unless somebody does it" speeches? Cassandra's heart was heavy as she thought about how her mother insinuated that JT was not a true man of God. No matter what JT had done, Cassandra had always believed he was a man of God, but what if her mother was right? What if JT made so many mistakes because he wasn't a true man of God? She stopped listening to her husband's message, and searched the "important people chairs" for Bishop Turner. Her eyes danced with joy as she spotted the bishop, and then leaned down and whispered to her mother, "I can't help it. I still wish that Bishop Turner had been my father. Why couldn't you have met him before he married Suzie?"

Mattie flinched. "Hush, girl, I'm trying to make sense of this fool's message."

Cassandra knew that her mother was not intently listening to JT. But she also knew that her mother hated when she talked about Bishop. So she leaned back in her seat and dreamed a little. Her father had died before she was born, but she didn't miss him. Bishop Turner had always been there for her, just like a daddy. So, every night she would pray for God to make Bishop her daddy. She didn't even mind if she had to share him with his two sons, just as long as he belonged to her also. As she grew older, she came to terms with the fact that Bishop would never be her father, and accepted his role as godfather in her life.

Bishop had introduced her to JT. He even came home early from his Caribbean vacation to marry them. There were days she knew with everything in her that she only held onto this marriage to please her godfather.

She turned back to her husband and listened as he prepared to close his sermon. *What happened to you, JT? What became of all your big dreams? What happened to us*? None of those questions were appropriate for the first lady of Faith Outreach Church, but her heart was full of them anyway. Even as her husband finished his sermon, walked down to where she sat, took her hand, and stood her up to plant a kiss on her lips, she wondered what had happened to the feelings that used to soar through her when he did this.

"What did you think of my sermon, baby?" JT asked.

"It was all right," she said as she pulled her hand from his, and made her way to the pulpit where Bishop Turner sat. Giving her godfather a tight hug, Cassandra sighed. "I've missed you. How can you stay away so long?"

"It was not on purpose, my sweet Cassandra. There are just too many fires to put out in the kingdom of God." The Bishop took her head in his hands and placed a delicate kiss on her forehead. "But I promise, not a day went by that I didn't think of you."

"Don't let Junior or Edward hear you say that. They would blow a gasket."

They linked arm in arm and strolled toward JT's office. "Don't you worry about my sons; they know that I take my responsibility as your godfather very seriously."

Bishop had always been a prominent figure in Cassandra's life. She knew he would do anything for her; that fact had always brought her comfort. Cassandra just wished that her husband took his responsibilities to her as seriously as her godfather did.

CHAPTER 2

Jimmy Littleton's skeletal frame slowly walked all the way home. No reason to hurry. He had no job, no family, and no big-bootie woman awaiting his return. He did have a gun though. And as he stood in front of his dilapidated, roof-'bout-to-cave-in house, with a forty-ounce swinging from his hand, he thought a bullet to the head might be just the buzz he was looking for.

"Hey, Jimmy," Charlie, his creepy, thick sideburn–wearing next-door neighbor, called out. "The police stopped by your place today. I guess you're done vacationing with us. 'Bout to run on back home to your nice comfy cell, huh?"

Jimmy tried to ignore him, but Creepy Charlie's clamorous laughter could be heard even as he walked into his house, toward the back bedroom.

Pulling his 9 mm from the three-legged night stand his mother bequeathed to him, he headed back downstairs toward the kitchen. A tuna sandwich would go good with his forty. Putting the gun on the counter, he opened the fridge. Covering his nose, he slammed the fridge as the smell of rotten tuna assaulted his nostrils. The refrigerator had stopped running again. Life sucked.

If he could find that lowlife, JT, and put him through a slow, painful, eye-gouging death, then maybe life would go better for him. After spending six years in prison for a crime he and JT committed, and not receiving one care package from the man who had collected a "get out of jail free" card from his silent lips, Jimmy needed to even the score. He'd spent the last nine years of his life searching for his old buddy. Okay, maybe he'd spent more time behind bars in the last nine years than on his search. But he did his best. And you can't knock the prison connection. They know how to find lowlifes. So it was odd that *his* lowlife remained hidden. Like he had stopped dealing with criminals all together. But Jimmy knew better than that. There was no such thing as rehabilitation.

Every day Jimmy woke, he imagined JT spending his money and laughing at him. Taking a swig from his bottle, he realized that he couldn't stand it anymore. The police were looking for him again. Probably mad about the convenience store he robbed last night. They might be a little upset about the way he tied those clerks up and left them in the back of the store. Why couldn't they just get over it? At least they found them. He could have shot them in the head. But he took the high road and acted like a Good Samaritan. Nobody was ever grateful. Everybody held a grudge. Even him.

That's why he couldn't go on, couldn't live another day with a grudge that was causing him to lose focus and mess up simple convenience store jobs. Now the police were on his back again.

He took another swig, picked up his gun, and headed to the living room. Turning on the TV, he decided to do something unusual. With a smile, he changed the channel, thinking how wonderful it would be for the police to come in his house and find him with his brains splattered out, and a sermon blaring.

He turned up the volume as he found the Word Channel. Even sinners at the end of their rope could find redemption. Isn't that what Christians always spouted? "Come to Jesus, He will save you."

An anniversary celebration was going on. Praise dancers filled the screen. When he was a kid, his mom had taken him to see *Swan Lake*. He still remembered how the ballerinas danced around, leotards flowing gracefully. Happy times. It had been all good when his mother had been alive. But cancer took her away, and the boogeyman took her place. His father did nothing but drink and abuse him. Thinking about the nightmare on Canal Street made Jimmy lift the gun to his head. He turned his attention back to the TV; wanted to hear some preacher spout off about the goodness of God while he blew his brains out. The pastor was taking his place behind the pulpit.

Jimmy lowered the gun and sat up. That was no pastor. The man standing before him was JT Thomas. His partner in crime. His enemy. He put the gun on the coffee table. Now he had better things to do than die. Anyway, he couldn't go before JT, now could he?

CHAPTER 3

JT walked into the kitchen with frowning and complaining lips. "Pork chops again?"

Dawg. Cassandra had forgotten she'd fixed pork chops last Sunday. "I could smother them, and boil some rice to go with them."

JT waved her off. "Just give me what you got. I have a meeting at the church that I need to get back to."

She turned back to her stainless steel stove and filled his plate with the baked macaroni and cheese, yams, green beans, and a pork chop over which she'd labored at seven o'clock that morning. JT was always hungry when he finished his sermon. She'd learned early on in their marriage that trying to prepare a meal after church wouldn't do. Her husband hated going hungry and would throw a fit if she tried to get out of cooking. She handed him his plate, fixed her own, then sat down at the kitchen table with him. The children had fallen to sleep on the drive home from church, so it was just she and JT at the dinner table. "I thought the men's meeting was cancelled?"

He shoved the mac and cheese in his mouth. He then

took a healthy bite out of the pork chop and continued to look down at his plate, as if he were in a race that required him to devour his food within the next two seconds.

"JT, did you hear me?" Cassandra asked.

Shoving green beans and yams in his mouth, he looked up. "Huh?"

Cassandra shook her head as she said, "When are you going to stop acting like your food is about to run away from you?"

He put his fork down and wiped his mouth. "You're the best cook I know, baby. I can't stop myself after I take the first bite."

"Well, just don't choke yourself."

JT laughed. "I've got too much work to do to choke to death."

"Which brings me back to my original question." Cassandra asked suspiciously, "I thought the men's meeting was cancelled for tonight."

"It was. I'm meeting with the choir tonight. We've got that musical coming up for Bishop Turner and I want to make sure they understand how important this is. You know my motto: nothing gets done, unless—"

"I know, I know. But why do you always have to be the somebody doing it?"

"I don't have time to argue with you right now, Sanni." He put on his jacket and bent down to kiss his wife on the forehead. "I won't be long. Have the boys wait up so I can put them to bed, okay?"

She grabbed his hand and said, "Sit back down for a minute, JT."

"Is it important, baby? I really need to get going,"

"I think it is. Can you have a seat for a minute?"

JT huffed, but sat back down. "Okay, now what's so important that it can't wait until I get back?"

"What's going on with you?"

"What do you mean? I don't understand the question," he said with a raised eyebrow.

She glided her hand across the top of his as she said, "You've become distant again. Like you were when . . ."

JT pulled his hand away and stood up. "Don't say it, Cassandra. I get so tired of you rehashing the past. There's nothing wrong with us. I just have an appointment I need to get to." He looked at his watch like the first President Bush had when he debated then Governor Clinton. "I'm already late. I'll talk to you about this later."

JT walked out of the door and Cassandra let him go. Her marriage was falling apart and she didn't know what to do. JT refused to talk about the very thing that Cassandra knew was still bothering him, even after all these years.

She stood up and removed the plates from the table, thinking that it just might be time to call a marriage counselor.

Driving down the street, JT smiled to himself. He had accomplished more than most men dreamed about. He was no longer the poor little kid whose mother was a junkie, selling her food stamps and whatever else she could to get money for her next high. No, he was somebody. He owned a Bentley, and he and his wife lived in a 7,000 square–foot home. A mini-mansion, if you will, and JT planned to have a full-fledged mansion within two years. God had come into his life, anointed him to preach, and given him a wife worthy of any preacher.

JT had to admit, Cassandra was all right. She was pretty enough with that smooth, chocolate skin and those deep dimples he loved. Her dainty little body would make any man thank God for small favors. Especially when it snuggled up to him on cold nights. She made sure their children were clean and fed. And when he got the itch, she took care of him also. But something was missing. It had to be.

His cell phone rang. He looked at the caller ID and then pushed the talk button. "Hey, what's up, baby?"

The caller said, "I was just wondering if I was going to see you tonight?"

He smiled lazily, like a man who'd been left a million dollars by a distant relative he'd never had to take to the grocery store, pick up medicine at the pharmacy for, or stop by to check in on every so often. "Where's your husband?" he asked.

"He took the kids to the movies—a double feature," she answered seductively.

Disappointment spread across JT's face. "I wish I could come see you, I really do. But I'm headed to a meeting right now. I wish you would have had him do that double feature yesterday."

"JT, you haven't called or come by here since I got out of the hospital. Are you trying to avoid me?"

"That's crazy talk, girl. You've only been home three weeks; you're not up to having visitors yet."

She screamed into the phone, "JT, if you don't get over here right now, I will call the church and tell them all about us."

"Calm down. Why are you so upset?"

"I'm not joking with you, JT. I need to see you right now."

He made a U-turn. "I'm on my way. I'll see you in a minute." He hung up the phone and then dialed another number. When it was answered he said, "I'm running a little late. I have to take care of something before I can get over there. Okay?"

The person on the other end of the phone said, "That's

too bad, baby. Well, I guess I'll just have to find something else to occupy my time."

"Read a book," JT replied. "You better not invite another man over there. Do you hear me?"

She laughed, "Whatever, JT."

"No, not whatever. Go get a book and I'll see you in an hour. Now I've got to go," he said, as he turned the corner onto a street with which he had become very familiar.

He pulled into the driveway, opened his cell phone, and punched in a few numbers. When the call was picked up he said, "Hey, it's me. Open the garage."

The garage door lifted, and JT pulled his Bentley inside. He got out of his car and shook his leg to straighten the creases from his three-hundred-dollar pants, then pushed the button to close the garage door. He took off his coat, and walked through the adjoining door, into the house of one of his deacons. But Deacon Benson wasn't at home; his wife Diane was waiting for JT in the living room.

"What took you so long?" Diane asked as JT moved toward her.

"Stop playing, Diane. I have to be somewhere in less than an hour. What's so important?"

Diane was seated on the couch, and next to her was a basinet. She stood up, bent over the basinet, and lifted the baby out of it. She handed the baby to JT and said, "I thought you would finally want to see your little girl. Lily has been waiting to meet her daddy."

"Hold up," he said as he handed the baby back to her. "Don't try to get nothing started, Diane. You know I'm not the father of your baby."

"You didn't even look at her. Don't you want to see if she looks like you?" Diane lifted the baby higher so JT could see her face. "Now, how can you say she isn't your baby?"

JT thought back, and realized with horrifying guilt that he had been in the vicinity when Diane had gotten pregnant. But he still wouldn't look at the little girl's face. "I think you need glasses, Diane. She looks like Deacon Benson."

"You didn't even look at her."

"Yes, I did."

She came closer to him and put her baby in his face. "You're lying, JT. This is your baby and you know it. Look at her!" she screamed.

For other reasons very close to his heart, JT didn't want to look at the little girl in front of him. But he turned his face toward the baby anyway. As he looked at her, he remembered the flutter in his stomach the day he first looked at his boys. He didn't feel anything right now, and took that as confirmation. He pushed Diane away from him and turned to leave. "I've got to go. I'll talk to you once you've regained your right mind. Obviously, having that baby has destroyed some of your brain cells."

"What about Lily, JT? You can't just walk away from your responsibilities."

"I don't have anything to do with this."

Diane sat down, holding her baby close to her as she began to sob.

JT wanted to go to her and comfort her, but the woman had just accused him of fathering her baby. He would never come within striking distance of her again. He put his coat back on and left without saying another word.

Driving down the street, JT thought about going home. But then he realized that he didn't want to get into another discussion with Cassandra. So he kept moving to his original destination. He pulled into the driveway where his meeting for the night would be held. He dialed the occupant's telephone number and asked her to raise her garage door. JT didn't like leaving his car exposed. He pulled into the garage, got out of the car, went into the house, and walked straight into the master bedroom. Vivian Sampson, the new choir director at his church, sat on the edge of her bed with a black negligee on. Her legs were crossed, revealing how long and sexy they were.

JT leaned against the bedroom door and licked his bottom lip. "Ms. Sampson, is your choir ready for the bishop's musical next month?"

Vivian put her hand on the pole of her canopy bed and struck a seductive pose that allowed JT a fuller view of her bountiful breasts. "Yes, Pastor, my choir is more than up for the challenge."

JT closed the bedroom door and stepped into a fire that more than consumed him. It left him weary and conflicted. By the time he left Vivian's bed to go into the bathroom and clean himself, his head was pounding. He opened her medicine cabinet and took out the Tylenol. But when he closed the cabinet door, he found himself staring at a monster's pockmarked face that laughed at him in the mirror.

Closing his eyes, he shook himself. He then slowly opened his eyes, praying that he would see a reflection of himself. But the monster in the mirror grew more hideous. The pockmarks on his forehead grew into horns and the greenish-grey eyes that looked like his darkened, as the sclerae reddened as if fire shot through them. JT backed away until his body was against the wall. He turned his head, not wanting to see the monster in the mirror again, because he knew deep in his gut that the monster was him. He slid to the floor and leaned against the sparkling white tub.

JT.

JT heard someone call his name. He searched the small bathroom but found no one. Then it struck him: he knew he was hearing the voice of God.

When you called out to Me, I delivered you. But you have forsaken Me. And I will deliver you no more.

Tears flowed down his cheeks as he accepted God's judgment. "What happened to me?" JT well remembered the day he'd called out to the Lord. He so badly had wanted out of the life he'd been forced to live, that he would have crawled all the way to heaven on bloody knees. "How did I get so far away from You, Lord?"

CHAPTER 4

June, 1993

Walking into his mother's house was like seeing an unwanted prophecy come true. He'd told her that shooting that stuff into her veins would kill her. Now, he stood over his mother's body. She was laying on the dirty orange carpet. As he leaned down to lift her in his arm, a roach crawled from under her. "Mama, wake up. Do you hear me, Mama?"

The lids of her eyes parted. Then he saw her eyes roll backward as her body went limp. "No, Mama, don't do this to me."

The needle she used to send her happy juice flowing through her body was on the ground next to her. The rope was still knotted and tied to her arm. JT shook his mother. "Wake up. Do you hear me? I said wake up."

But her body was stiff. She was gone. He took the rope from around her arm, put her needle in the trash, then picked up his mother and gently placed her on the couch. He didn't cry as he called for an ambulance. He had practiced for this event ever since he was nine years old, when his mother first put that needle of death in her arm. He was twenty-two now, and all cried out about the sunken-in cheeks that had destroyed the beauty of the woman who used to reside in his mother's body. All cried out about the high school graduation and subsequent wedding she had missed. She had been so high, she hadn't realized how many important events in her son's life she would miss. One after the other.

He picked up plates from the floor, and scraped the half-eaten contents into the trash. He threw dirty cups and empty boxes of frozen food into the trash as well, tied the trash bag, and tossed it into the dumpster out back. He couldn't give her a peaceful life, couldn't stop her from shooting poison into her body, but he could give her a bit of dignity in death.

When the paramedics arrived and asked him what had happened, JT told them, "I don't know. When I came in the house she was laying on the couch like that. I thought she was asleep, but I couldn't wake her."

The paramedics exchanged glances, but said nothing. They wheeled his mother's body out of her rented home. JT closed the door behind them and walked away without looking back. There were no memories in that house he would cherish. Christmas and birthdays had gone unnoticed. No scrapbooks of laughing children or smiling parents would be retrieved from his childhood home. His memories of this place were as bleak and dirty as the carpet on which he'd found his mother.

Numbly, he got in his car and headed home. Mona was all he had now. He'd married his prom date after she called four weeks after prom claiming to be pregnant. JT and Mona had not been a couple during high school. He'd dated Erica Swell. Erica had been a cheerleader and he had been a football player. Erica was a Christian girl with plans to save herself for marriage. JT had tried his best to wait, but during their senior year Mona kept making promises—telling him what she would do for him. So he broke up with Erica before the prom, figuring he would be able to get back with her once he'd had his fun with Mona. But Mona got pregnant, and JT began having dreams of a little girl calling him Daddy. He did the honorable thing and married Mona three months after he graduated from high school.

Mona lost the baby right after they married. His mother doubted if she had truly been pregnant in the first place, and used that as her excuse not to show up for his wedding. Sometimes, JT also wondered if Mona had played him. But he'd already lost Erica and given up a football scholarship, so the last thing he wanted confirmed was that it was all for nothing. He'd gotten a job as a custodian and made the best of his life. He'd even become fond of Mona and was hoping that she would get pregnant again, soon. So it was with a heavy heart that he drove home to his wife, looking for comfort.

What he found when he arrived home was the opposite of comfort. Well, somebody was being comforted, it just wasn't him. JT opened the back door and heard the sound of lovemaking coming from his bedroom. Stunned and already in a grieving state, he closed the door and sat down on the stoop outside. He figured he would wait until they were finished, then go inside, get his gun out of the closet, and shoot them.

Jimmy Littleton, JT's friend from high school, pulled up behind his car and jumped out. "What's doing, man?"

JT didn't respond. He put his head in his hand and let it slide backward through his high top fade.

"What's wrong, JT? Why you acting all numb?" Jimmy asked.

"My mother died today." He looked toward the back of

his house and added, "Oh yeah, and Mona is inside have sex with someone. I'm just waiting out here until they finish so I can kill them. You got any bail money?"

"No way, man. You kidding me?"

JT shook his head and ran his hand through his fade again.

Jimmy grabbed his friend's arm and pulled him off the stoop. "You're coming with me."

JT shook him off. "Naw, man. I'm waiting right here. I want them to see my face when that dude is finished having his way with my wife."

"Man, do you know whose car that is?" Jimmy pointed at the black Camaro boldly parked in front of JT's house.

JT gave Jimmy a dumbfounded look, and then shook his head again. "Nope, but I'm sure I'll find out when I shoot him."

Jimmy grabbed his arm again and pulled him toward his car. "Fool, that is Lester Grayson's car. The way I see it, if he is in there with your wife, let him have her or he'll kill you and take her anyway." Jimmy kept pulling JT. "Now come on, let's go."

JT knew all about Lester Grayson. He was the kingpin around town. He made his money off the weaknesses of people like his mother. That fancy Camaro and the Ford Explorer Lester drove around town like a big man had been bought by dead people. Dead people that Lester had murdered with his gun or with his dope. JT walked over to the Camaro and kicked it. The alarm on the car went off.

"Okay, JT, you've had your fun." Jimmy pulled him toward his car, opened the passenger door, and pushed JT in. Jimmy ran to the other side and jumped in. They sped off just as JT's front door opened and an angry Lester ran out with his 9 mm at the ready.

CHAPTER 5

"**D**id you see how that fool ran out of your house with his pants falling down?" Jimmy laughed as he hit the steering wheel.

"Yeah," JT told him. "If it weren't my life, it would almost be funny."

Jimmy turned to his friend. "Look, man, don't sweat it. Mona's been cheating on you since you got with her. We all wondered why you married her in the first place."

He wondered how come no one had bothered to inform him that his wife was the welcome mat for the city of New Orleans. He leaned the passenger seat back and closed his eyes. He'd given up a college scholarship and the girl he'd loved since ninth grade to marry Mona. And she repaid him by sleeping with the man that sold poison to his mother.

Jimmy drove JT around town until it got dark. He then pulled up in front of a drug house on Canal Street. He opened his glove compartment and pulled out two guns, handed one to JT, and said, "Let's do this."

JT put the gun back in the glove compartment. "Man, what are you talking about? Do what?"

"Don't you want to get even with Lester for messing around with Mona?"

"Sure I do. But what does that have to do with me picking up that gun?"

Jimmy pointed in the direction of an old dilapidated house. "That's one of his major crack houses. If we hit it, I guarantee ol' Lester will hurt a lot more than he did when you kicked his car. Now what do you say?"

JT thought of his mother stretched out on that dirty floor, needle next to her body. He thought about the sounds his wife made while laying with another man. He pulled the gun out of the glove compartment. "Let's do it."

They walked onto the porch and banged on the door a couple times. One of Lester's soldiers came to the door demanding, "What y'all want?"

Steve-O was at the door. Jimmy knew him from around the way. "Steve-O, man, what's up? We need to get on. You gon' help us or what? We got the money."

Steve-O gave them a gold-toothed grin as he opened the door. Jimmy could see by the bulge in his jacket that he was packing. So he quickly scanned the room to see if any of his boys were house-sitting with him. When he only saw a couple of crackheads on the floor too busy getting high to notice them, he whipped out his gun and cracked Steve-O across his head, knocking him to the ground. "Get his piece," Jimmy told JT.

When JT finished patting Steve-O down he'd retrieved two guns and a pocket knife.

"You think you gon' get away with this. Man, Lester gon' kill y'all," Steve-O stated.

Steve-O got smacked in the mouth with the butt of JT's

gun just for mentioning Lester's name. "Shut up. Now get up and get us the money, or you'll be too dead to tell Lester what went on here tonight."

Steve-O was bad, but he wasn't crazy bad. So he pulled out his money bag and handed over fifty thousand dollars. "Thanks, man. I'll check you later," Jimmy told him as he and JT backed out of the house. They hit three more of Lester's houses. Jimmy didn't want Lester to feel all the pain. Sometimes innocent bystanders have to learn that life sucks just like the rest of the world. At least, that's what Jimmy told JT to explain why they were stealing a car after hitting their third house.

"I don't know, man. I don't mind wronging Lester, but the person who owns this car probably has a family to feed. Probably has to get up and go to work in the morning."

"Yeah, you right. This Buick is a family man's car. You wouldn't catch no hustler in it, that's for sure." They drove away from the Buick, and then Jimmy spotted a tinted out Deville with hydraulics two blocks away. He turned to JT and asked, "Is it okay if we borrow that one?"

"Man, whatever," JT told him. Unfortunately for JT, Jimmy wasn't finished. They stopped at a Wal-Mart and bought two ski masks, then hit the fourth house. Why hadn't Jimmy been smart enough to pick up the ski masks before they hit house number one?

This was JT's first, second, third, and fourth felony. And he was already tiring of the criminal life; kind of wished that some crime-stopper would put an end to his car jacking, dope house–robbing spree. But he never wished for Lester to be at the fourth house waiting on them, or that he would take a bullet as he ran like Edwin C. Moses going for the gold. As he dove through the window of the *rented* Deville he had one prevailing thought: How had Jimmy, the guy who would rob his mama and still sleep as if he were lying on clouds, the mastermind behind this crime spree, beat him to the car? And how come he didn't have a bullet in his behind?

"He got me," JT hollered as Jimmy sped down the street.

Pop, pop, pop. Bullets hit the car.

Jimmy floored the peddle, trying to get out of Lester's way. Once they had put distance between them and lead poisoning, Jimmy said, "Let's just ride until morning, so we can get as far away from this place as possible."

"I need to get to a hospital, man," JT screamed at him.

"If I take you to a hospital in this town, you won't be attending your mother's funeral, you'll be having your own."

"I don't care," JT yelled. "I need to get this bullet out of me." He grabbed Jimmy's collar. "This was all your idea. Help me, man. Don't just let me bleed to death while you ride out of here."

"Okay, okay. But no hospital," Jimmy said as he turned into the Holiday Inn in the French Quarter. Once they were checked into the room, Jimmy dug the bullet out of JT's upper thigh with his pocket knife, then wrapped a sheet around his leg.

"You know they're going to charge you for this sheet," JT said through clenched teeth.

Jimmy laughed. "Yeah, they probably will charge Charles Dewitt for tearing up the sheets and filling them with blood."

"Who's Charles Dewitt?"

"Guess who left his credit card in the glove compartment of the Deville?"

"You stole that guy's credit card?"

Jimmy laughed again. "How stupid do you think this

guy is—leaving a credit card in a car that anybody could steal at anytime? Dummy."

Since they were too paranoid to sleep, they spent the night counting money. One night of robbing had netted them two hundred and fifty thousand dollars. Jimmy scooped up some of the money and walked around the room. "I always knew there was a God," he said, kissing his loot.

"Don't mock God, Jimmy. Erica used to tell me that God hears and sees all. So, since I'm already a thief, I'd rather not be seen as someone who mocks God also."

Jimmy waved him off. "Please. The man upstairs ain't thinking about us. And He sure don't care about us robbing a lowlife like Lester Grayson."

JT laid down and tried to rest his eyes, but the sound of someone walking on their floor caused his eyes to open. He grabbed his gun and asked Jimmy to check it out.

A drunken couple staggered to their room after doing the night New Orleans'–style, no doubt. Jimmy leaned against the door and lightly tapped the gun against his forehead. "Man, will you get some sleep. Lester don't know where we are."

"Maybe we should have rode out of this city. Stopping at this hotel for the night was stupid," JT said.

Jimmy smiled. "Naw, it was brilliant. Lester will think we left town, and that will give us the chance to hit one more place in the morning."

JT shook his head. "Not me. Count me out, Jimmy. Robbing people is not what I want to do with the rest of my life. Now, I went along with what we did tonight because it helped to relieve some tension, with my mother dying on me like she did and my wife cheating on me. But count me out of the rest of your schemes."

"I can't live on no hundred and twenty-five thousand. I

need a score that will get me through some years. Maybe help me start a business of my own. Buy a franchise or something."

JT could understand goals and dreams. He'd had a few before he married Mona and threw his life away. "Like I said, count me out."

CHAPTER 6

They left the hotel at about nine the next morning. As they drove down the street, they made plans for their new life, trying to decide whether they'd go to Texas, Mississippi, or Tennessee. But before they could get out of town, Jimmy pulled the stolen car up to the Bank of Trust in downtown New Orleans.

"Why you stopping?" JT asked.

"Man, I got to pee," Jimmy told him. He pulled his gun from under his seat and slid it in his pants' pocket.

"Why you need a gun to go pee?"

"Shut up, man. You don't want none of this. Fine, I won't split my take with you. Just get your butt behind this wheel and drive me out of here when I come running out of this bank."

JT rolled his eyes as he scooted over to the driver's side. What could he do? He'd pulled off four burglaries the night before with Jimmy. He wasn't going in the bank with him, so fine, if he had to drive that knucklehead away from this place, he would do it. But this was it; he was done with Jimmy Littleton. If he had to walk the twenty-five miles across Lake Ponchatrain to get out of this town, he'd do it. He was done with New Orleans. Done with Mona, and done with friends like Jimmy.

JT tapped his fingers on the dashboard, looking round about him, making sure the coast was clear. His pager was going off again. He pulled it off his belt loop and looked at the number. It was who he thought; Mona had been blowing up his pager all night. Probably figured out that he'd caught her in the act when she saw that his car was in the driveway. Then an idea struck him. If he had his own car, he wouldn't have to ride with stick-'em-up Jimmy. There was a pay phone on the walk across from his car. He jumped out of the car to call Mona, to find out if the coast was clear.

Pain shot up his leg as he limped to the phone. He dialed Mona's number. When she answered the phone, he said, "Why you keep paging me?"

"I am your wife, JT. I have a right to know why you didn't come home."

"I did come home."

Silence.

Something was up. The Mona he knew would be trying to talk herself out of the mess she willingly stepped into. He was sure that she already knew he'd come home last night; she had to have seen his car in the driveway.

Cutting through his thoughts, Mona said, "When will you be home?"

Why did she let that go so easy? Why wasn't she asking who he was sleeping with? Any other woman would have thought he must have been in bed with someone in order not to come home all night. But Mona didn't care. Matter of fact, JT would put money on it that she was probably sitting in the house with that lowlife, Lester, trying to get him to come home so she could start wearing black and letting her mascara run. He hung up on his loving wife, got back in the car and looked at his watch. Jimmy had been in that bank seven minutes. What was he doing, opening up an account?

The car quit running. "Oh, no you don't." JT pumped the gas and started it again. When he looked up, two police cars sped past him and pulled up in front of the bank. JT almost peed his pants when he saw the officers jump out of their cars and run into the bank with guns drawn. He eased out of his spot and made sure to do the speed limit as he turned the corner. Sweat trickled from his forehead as the police car sped by him again. He saw Jimmy's side profile in the back of the car. His lips were moving, and JT imagined that he was spilling his guts to the cops trying to plead his time down.

JT prayed like he'd never prayed in his life. He prayed harder than he did when Erica had taken him to her church so that God would take the lust out of his heart so he'd forget about Mona and stay with the woman he loved. Crossing Lake Ponchatrain he told God, "If you get me out of this, I swear I'll serve You."

JT was tired. He'd lived this go-nowhere life for twenty-two years too long. His mother had been a junkie who never cared about what concerned him. He hadn't held a job in months and had no prospects in sight. He needed a new life. A chance. He wondered if what Erica told him about God sitting on His throne just waiting to forgive and forget was really true. He wanted, no, needed something different than anything he'd ever known.

He kept driving, praying. He still wasn't sure where he was going, or what he would do. Well, he did know that he needed to get to a hospital. But he needed to be far away from New Orleans so no one would connect his bullet wound with the multiple drug house robberies he and Jimmy pulled off. So he just kept driving and hoping that the bleeding had stopped for good. Entering Alabama, JT realized he'd been so caught up in his prayers that he'd forgotten to check the gas gauge. Unfortunately, it wasn't until the "check gauge" light came on that he even thought about gas. With no gas station in sight, the car puttered into an empty lot. He stumbled out of the car, screaming in pain each time his left leg connected with the pavement. Hadn't God heard his plea for help?

Putting his hands on top of his head, he stood in the middle of the parking lot. That's when he noticed he had a fever. His head was hotter than a baker's oven. His vision was blurring. But he could see the church building in front of him. A man stepped out of the building and walked toward him. Maybe it was two men. Or maybe it was one gigantic man that kept spreading and splitting in two.

His legs couldn't hold him any longer. They wobbled and JT fell to the ground. Just before his eyes closed, he saw the man standing over him, heard him say something about the hospital, and silently thanked God for sending someone to help him.

CHAPTER 7

November, 2009

Pulling himself off the floor, JT went back to the mirror. The same handsome face he'd seen for thirty-seven years stared back at him. The hideous monster was gone. Or was it still inside him, sitting back, waiting for the most opportune moment to rear its ugly head again?

"JT, what's taking you so long in there?"

JT's eyes widened as he realized he was still at Vivian Sampson's house. When would this nightmare end?

"JT?"

"I'm coming," he told her as he splashed cold water on his face and stepped into the bedroom.

Vivian was stretched out on her bed like she was doing one of those Hot Girls 900– number commercials. She patted the bed. "Come over here."

And for the first time in years he felt conviction. Felt disgust. Felt the bile rise up in his throat and begin to choke him. He turned and ran to the bathroom, fell down on his knees, and hugged the toilet.

"What's wrong? You got the flu or something?" Vivian asked as she followed him into the bathroom.

JT couldn't answer her. He was too busy barfing up his dinner. Too busy getting a taste of how his actions must feel to God. Too busy feeling sorry about not being a strong enough man to resist temptation.

Vivian flushed the toilet as JT got up and rinsed out his mouth. He sat on the bench at the foot of her bed putting on his socks and shoes. Stepping toward him, Vivian put her arms around him and asked, "What's going on? I thought you were hanging out with me for a little while today?"

He couldn't look at her. He stood, put on his suit jacket, and adjusted his tie.

"JT, do you hear me talking to you?"

He turned toward her, but kept his eyes averted. "I've got to go home, Vivian."

"You sick?" She came toward him again, putting her hands on his stomach. "Baby, I can take care of you."

Removing her hands from his stomach, JT told her, "I'm not interested, okay, Vivian. I just want to go home to my wife."

Her hands went to her hips. Sista's neck weaved and bobbed. "Oh, so that's it, huh? You think you can come over here and jump in my bed, then after you get what you want, just run home to your wife like I'm nothing?"

"It's not like that." He pointed to her bathroom, wanting to tell her how afraid he was of the monster he saw in that mirror. But he knew she would just think that he'd lost his mind, so he said, "I just threw up in there. I'm not good company for anybody right now."

She brushed her hand across his cheek. "You don't have to leave; I can make you feel better," she persisted seductively.

He was tempted to stay, just climb back in bed with her

and enjoy her company. But if he saw that hideous monster in the mirror again when he finished with Vivian, he would probably drop dead of a heart attack. And how would that look, for a married pastor to be found dead in the master bath of one of his single church members? He just couldn't do it. So he walked away from her.

"Don't leave." She ran to him and put her arms around him. "Stay with me."

Pulling her arms from around his waist he told her, "I don't belong here."

She went wild then, striking and clawing him. He grabbed her hands and she kicked him in the groin. He bowed low; not to Jesus, but to regain his breath after shock waves of pain shot through his body from Vivian's assault.

"What's wrong with you?" he asked when he could speak again.

"I'm sorry, baby. Please don't be mad." Vivian ran to the bathroom, got some tissue, and brought it back to JT. "Here, put this against your face. It should stop bleeding in a minute."

Horrified at the thought of going home with inexplicable scratches on his face, JT went into the bathroom and examined his face. Vivian had gotten him good. Three huge whelps trailed down the right side of his face. He turned on the faucet and splashed some water on his face. His cheek wasn't bleeding anymore, but the white meat showed through one of the whelps.

Vivian walked into the bathroom. She had taken off her clothes again. "Come back to bed, baby. I'll kiss your cheek and make it all better."

This nut needs a session with Dr. Phil. She has to be bipolar. "I'm leaving, Vivian." He rushed past her so she wouldn't have another chance to attack him.

Vivian screamed at him. "I'll get you, JT. Do you hear me? I'll make you pay for the way you've treated me."

Cassandra put her children to bed, then went to her bedroom for some quiet time with the Lord. She picked up her Bible and turned to Proverbs 31. It was her earnest prayer to be like this woman the Bible described as being so virtuous. But it was obvious that she didn't measure up. Her Bible read,

> *The heart of her husband safely trust in her, so that he shall have no need of spoil.*

And hadn't those women JT fooled around with spoiled any hopes of a trusting and loving relationship with her husband?

She was tired of pretending. Tired of trying to make this farce of a marriage work. Sometimes Cassandra even wondered about God. After all, she had waited on God. She hadn't been like so many of her Christian friends, running up to the first man who walked into the church and proclaiming that God told her he was supposed to be her husband. No, she spent her lonely nights in prayer, trying to grow closer to God, to discover His will for her life. But God had brought JT into her life, and she was struggling to forgive Him for that.

As tired as Cassandra was, she knew she still needed to think of Jerome and Aaron. Her sons were so young. How could she tear them away from their father?

She put aside her Bible and got on her knees to pray. She really needed some direction. Closing her eyes she began, "Lord, I have tried to trust You. But I've got to be honest; this thing with JT is taking me past my endurance.

"You know that I was not looking for a man when You brought JT into my life. I just wanted to grow closer to

You. So, I'm having a hard time understanding why You would give him to me, if he wasn't going to treat me right."

She exhaled and wiped the tears that had fallen on her face. "I love You, Lord, and I love my husband. I just don't know if I like him anymore. I need Your help. I need You to mend my heart so that I can be this Proverbs 31 woman."

After ending her prayer, she got off the floor and went to check on her children. Jerome and Aaron were still asleep. She knew that Aaron wouldn't sleep much longer, he never did. She would be so glad when that one learned to sleep through the night.

She went into the kitchen to fix herself some hot chocolate. As she was stirring the mix into the hot water she'd boiled in the microwave, the telephone rang. She picked up the receiver with one hand and kept stirring her cocoa with the other. Cassandra answered with her usual greeting. "Praise the Lord."

The woman cleared her throat. "Uh, hello First Lady, this is Diane Benson."

"How are you doing, Diane?"

The church had more than three thousand members. Therefore, they had numerous elders, deacons, and ministers assigned to handle parishioner concerns, but every now and then, one of them would get a hold of their home number and call for prayer or for information about the different ministries within the church. But Diane was the wife of one of their deacons. Cassandra received calls from the women in leadership, usually because they worked on church committees. However, Diane didn't work on any committees, so Cassandra was a little confused about the call.

"I don't know how to tell you this," Diane began.

Cassandra gripped the telephone tighter. Instinct told her to sit down.

"When I first came to your church, I really wanted to get closer to God. But . . . but JT, I mean, Pastor Thomas . . ."

"Go on," Cassandra encouraged when Diane's voice trailed off.

"I guess there's no easy way to say this. So I should just come right out with it. I've been sleeping with your husband."

This revelation didn't shock Cassandra. Many women had slept with her husband. She'd moved past shock ability years ago. When she responded to Diane her words were calm. "How long has this been going on?"

"About a year." Diane then added, "Anyway, the thing is . . ." She hesitated for a moment, took a deep breath, and said, "The baby girl I just had belongs to JT."

CHAPTER 8

When JT walked into his bedroom, Cassandra was throwing clothes into a suitcase. "You going someplace?"

"Nope," she said without looking his way. She walked into the closet, pulled down a few of his suits, and threw them onto the bed, then opened the dresser drawers that contained his socks and undergarments.

"What are you doing?" he asked when he finally caught on that his clothes were those being packed.

"Giving you your freedom, so you can see as many women as your heart desires." She looked at him and added, "You just won't have the added bonus of me waiting up, wondering where you are or who you're with. Because I don't care anymore."

"I'm not leaving my home." He started taking his clothes out of the suitcase. "What's gotten into you? Why are you acting like this?" *That psycho must have called his house*, he thought, then quickly said, "Look, Sanni, you can't believe everything Vivian says. The woman is crazy, and not just your average crazy—she needs to be locked up."

Cassandra stopped pulling his underwear out of the drawer and turned to face him. "Who is Vivian?"

"Isn't that why you're throwing my clothes all over the place, because Vivian called and filled your head with lies?"

Now she saw the scratches on his face. "Is that who gave you those scratches? This Vivian woman?"

He touched the scars on his face, but didn't answer her.

Then it hit her, and anger flooded her soul. "Vivian Sampson, the choir director?"

He lowered his head, refusing to look at her.

She threw his socks and boxers at his head, wishing she had something heavier, like a hammer. She would hit him with it over and over again; until she beat all the fool out of him. "You're no good, JT. And I want you out of here tonight." She stormed past JT. He tried to stop her by grabbing her arm, but she pulled away. Then she turned back to him and said, "Her name is Diane."

"What?"

She still had a pair of his boxers in her hand. She handed them to JT. "The woman who just had your baby called me tonight. It wasn't Vivian, it was Diane Benson, and just so you know, I gave her Bishop Turner's number and suggested that she tell him what you did." She walked away from him and went into her son, Aaron's, room.

JT was too stunned to move. He closed his eyes and let out a deep sorrowful groan. He turned and followed his wife.

Aaron was stirring. She picked him up. "You looking for your mommy? Huh? Yeah, I know what you want." She sat down in the rocking chair and nursed her son.

JT leaned against the doorpost wishing he could take a thousand wrongs back. He felt as though God had forsaken him, and now his life was falling apart. Then he remembered the story of King Hezekiah in the second book of Kings. The Lord sent Prophet Isaiah to tell him that he would die from the sickness he was afflicted with. But Hezekiah didn't just accept his death sentence; he turned his face to the wall and prayed, reminding God of his faithfulness. And God heard his prayers and healed him.

JT didn't have much faithfulness to remind God of, but maybe if he reminded Cassandra of the love they had once shared, she would forgive him. Falling to his knees, JT began to weep. He wasn't crying out to God though; his tears were for his family. He didn't want to lose his wife, so he begged like a man caught in the act.

Cassandra shushed him. "Get out of here, JT. I'm trying to feed my son."

JT wouldn't let it go. He couldn't let her go. How could he stand behind his pulpit and tell others to hold onto their marriage while he was separated from his wife? He crawled to her and put his head on her lap. "Forgive me," he begged.

"How could you do this to us? I'll never forgive you for what you've done to me." Cassandra removed his head from her lap, stood with her son, and carried him back to his crib. She buttoned her shirt before turning to face her husband.

"I'll never cheat on you again, Sanni. You've got to believe me. I don't want to lose my family." *Why was God doing this to him?*

Rolling her eyes, she turned and walked out of Aaron's room.

JT stood and ran after her. In the hall he caught up with her and grabbed her arm. "Okay, Sanni. You do have reason to be angry, I'll give you that."

She put her index finger in his face. "I've got two things to be angry about, JT. Vivian *and* Diane. Oh, but wait a minute. I have another thing to be angry about: Diane's baby."

He shook his head. "I swear to you, Sanni, I didn't get that woman pregnant."

Rolling her eyes in disgust, she asked, "Then why did she call me?"

"It probably wasn't Diane at all, it was probably Vivian. The woman is nuts, baby."

"Why would Vivian call me if you're not fooling around with her?"

He stepped away from his wife and ran his hands through his hair. "Okay, I'm going to tell you the truth. I went over to Vivian's house tonight to go over the songs for Bishop Turner's special event."

Cassandra laughed, "Oh, that's it, JT. I am sick to death of your lying and cheating. You're supposed to be a man of God, but I see now that you are not. You are getting out of my house tonight!"

He grabbed her arm and told her, "I pay the note on this house, my dear wife. Let's not forget that I'm the one who made it possible for you to have this grand house."

She pulled her arm out of JT's grasp as she told him, "I never asked for this house or anything else you gave me. All I ever wanted was a faithful husband."

"Okay, okay," JT said in an agitated manner. "You're right. I slept with Vivian. Is that what you wanted to hear? Do you feel better now that you know the truth?"

Shaking her head, she turned away from him and stormed down the stairs. He followed her, willingly walking into the fire. He had to get it all out. Let her know everything that happened to him tonight. Had to let her know why he would never cheat on her again.

But Cassandra was finished, signing off, turning in her notice. She picked up the telephone and dialed 911. When the operator answered, she said, "I need the police. My husband came home with scratches on his face. When I asked him about it, he got agitated and grabbed my arm."

"Hand me that phone," JT angrily yelled.

"Do you hear how angry he sounds, I really need help— he might just resort to hitting me next." Cassandra covered the receiver, then turned to JT and said, "They want the address. I suggest you get your things and leave before they get here, unless you want to be on the news for domestic violence."

"You win this round, Sanni. I'll get my stuff and go to a hotel for the night. But this isn't over. We aren't over," he said just before he backed away from her, grabbed his suitcase, and then left the house.

CHAPTER 9

Although he didn't want to do it, JT was forced to flee from his home and check into the Marriott Hotel. He tossed and turned all night long just thinking about how bad it would look to his congregation once they found out he was estranged from his wife. He couldn't understand why Cassandra was being so pigheaded about the whole thing. She'd never reacted this way before; but then he remembered that God had forsaken him. He then had a thought that chilled him to the bone; had God been the one keeping his marriage together all these years? So would his marriage now disintegrate just as his relationship with God had? JT tried to get back to sleep, but he was plagued by these thoughts and, consequently, didn't get any rest.

By the time JT arrived at his office the next day, he was worn out. He sat behind his desk and opened his Bible. His life might be falling apart, but he still had to do Wednesday night Bible Study and preach Sunday's message. He pulled out a notepad and pen, and started jotting down notes. For the last three weeks he'd talked to his congregation about faith and works. Maybe he'd talk to them about regrets and second chances this week.

A knock on his office door pulled his attention from his sermon. "Yes?"

Mrs. Marks, his elderly secretary, opened the door and told him, "Vivian Sampson wants to see you. I told her you couldn't—"

"He'll see me," Vivian told Mrs. Marks as she pushed by her.

JT put his pen down with a look of annoyance on his face. "Ms. Sampson, this is not a good time for me."

"Oh, so it's Ms. Sampson now is it?"

JT had the decency to look embarrassed, as Mrs. Marks turned up her nose and closed his office door. "What do you want, Vivian? I've got work to do."

She sat on his desk. "What do I want? Let's see, I could want to talk with you about the choir." Looking at him with a taunting smile she continued. "Some of my choir members aren't living right. What should I do about that, Pastor?"

"Look, Vivian, I don't have time to play with you."

Ignoring him, she continued, "Or I could talk with you about Bishop Turner's celebration. What songs do you want the choir to sing for the good bishop?"

JT stood, walked over to his door, and opened it. "I don't have time for games, Ms. Sampson. When you have a legitimate reason to see me, please schedule an appointment with my assistant."

"You gon' get enough of dismissing me," she told him as she walked through the door in a huff.

Looking pointedly at his secretary, JT said, "Mrs. Marks, please make sure I'm not disturbed again. I have to finish this sermon."

"I'm sorry, Pastor, but you do have another visitor. He said he would wait all day to see you if he had to."

Rolling his eyes JT asked, "Who is it?"

Jimmy Litteton stepped from behind the door and greeted JT. "Would you be able to spare a few moments for an old friend?"

At that moment, JT would have rather had Vivian back in his office, taunting him. Jimmy looked haggard and worn out—like life had put a Mike Tyson kind of whuppin' on him. JT knew he was somewhat to blame for the meagerness of the man in front of him, but he smiled graciously and invited Jimmy to have a seat in his office.

"I see that wound didn't heal well," Jimmy said, pointing at JT's leg as he limped toward his seat.

JT stopped. He'd tried with everything in him to forget the night he had lost his mother and his woman, and then became a thief. But Jimmy was back in his world reminding him of how low he had once sunk. He wouldn't go back there. He continued to his seat and asked, "So what have you been doing with yourself? It's been a long time."

"Yeah, it's been fifteen years, three months, and two days since I last saw you."

JT stopped smiling. "Look, man, I know I should have written or put some money on your books or something . . ." He had no excuse, so his words kind of trailed off.

Jimmy exposed his crooked teeth as he asked, "Why do you think you should have put some money on my books? Just because I went to prison on a crime we both committed and you were left with all the money?"

JT held up a hand. "Now, wait a minute, Jimmy. I didn't tell you to rob that bank. Matter of fact, I asked you not to do it. But you weren't listening to me. You got greedy; that's why you ended up in prison."

Jimmy exploded as he stood and got in JT's face. "Everything I did that night was for you. It was your sorry behind that was moping around because your junkie mother had just OD'd and your cheating wife was giving her loving away to the dope man. You remember how it went down and don't try to pretend like you don't."

Honestly, JT told him, "For the last fifteen years I've made myself forget everything about those times."

"Well, good ol' Jimmy is here to remind you." He looked toward heaven and said, "Lookie here, Lord. I finally found a purpose in life." Laughing, he headed for the door.

"Wait a minute. You didn't tell me why you stopped by. What do you want?" JT asked.

"Don't you have a sermon to live, I mean, write?" He opened the door, and as he walked out he told JT, "I'll be in touch, man. You better believe ol' Jimmy gon' stay in touch with you."

Yeah, he had a sermon to write. The trouble was, nothing was sticking. He couldn't put anything of substance on paper. He'd never had trouble writing a sermon before. But, of course, that was before God decided to leave him with his sins.

JT had always thought of himself as self-reliant, but now he was beginning to see that without God, he was nothing. He put his head on his desk and let out a guttural moan.

"Are you all right, Pastor?" Mrs. Marks asked, standing in the doorway.

He tilted his head sideways but didn't lift it from the desk. Let's see; his wife had thrown him out, his mistress was stalking him, his ex-partner in crime showed up after fifteen years just to torment him; and oh yeah, God had forsaken him. "No, I'm not all right."

"Is there anything I can do?"

He looked at his secretary. She was a really sweet lady and he didn't want to burden her, so he said, "No. Don't worry about it, I'll be all right."

"Okay then. I just came in to tell you that Bishop Turner is on the phone."

JT shook his head, stood up, and grabbed his keys. He couldn't deal with the bishop right now. "Tell him I had to leave and I will call him back later."

When he got to his car, he let out another guttural moan. All four of his tires had been slashed. He couldn't even call the police. JT didn't know if the psycho he'd slept with or the madman he'd committed armed robbery with had slashed his tires—either way, it wouldn't be good press.

CHAPTER 10

Cassandra was in the front yard playing catch with Jerome when JT's cab pulled into the driveway. JT had promised his son that he would play catch with him, but he'd been so busy with church business and the other stuff he had no business doing that he'd neglected to make time for promises he'd made to his son.

Cassandra's brow raised as he walked toward them.

No sense lying; he'd done enough of that. "Someone slashed my tires," JT said as he looked around the yard. He asked, "Where's Aaron?"

"My mom has him for the afternoon."

"Oh," was all JT said in response.

Jerome ran to his father. "Daddy, play with me. Throw the ball."

He put down his briefcase, rolled up his sleeve, and took the ball from Cassandra's hand. She left them in the front yard and went back inside the house. He threw the ball with Jerome for twenty minutes, then went into the house. He asked if he could shower and change his clothes. Cassandra rolled her eyes, but nodded her approval.

JT had only taken a few of his clothes to the hotel the night before, so most of his things were still in the closet and in his dresser drawer. He took a shower, put on a pair of sweats, and went back downstairs to find his wife in the kitchen. "You still haven't asked me how my tires got slashed," he said.

Putting a pot of rice on the stove, Cassandra said, "Why should I ask when I know I'm not going to hear the truth?"

"That's just it, Sanni, I want to tell you the truth. I don't want us to have anymore secrets."

She harrumphed.

"I'm serious, baby. I want our marriage to work. I know I've messed up, but don't give up on me. We can work this out."

"Okay then." She wiped her hands on the dish towel and sat down at the table across from her husband. "How did your tires get slashed?"

He noticed that she didn't seem all that enthused about hearing his story, but he trudged on anyway. He told her about Vivian acting a fool in his office, then about Jimmy Littleton. He even told her about the robberies they'd committed years ago. He told her everything, only leaving out the minor detail of his marriage to Mona. He'd carry that one to his grave. But he would come clean about everything else.

When he was finished, Cassandra asked him, "So that's how you got that limp?"

"Yeah," he admitted, shamefaced. "I was too embarrassed to tell you I got shot during a robbery, so I just never talked to you about what happened to my leg."

"Why are you telling me all this now?"

"I want you to pray for me, Sanni. I know you can get a prayer through to God, so talk to Him for me."

She stood up. With sadness in her eyes, she told him, "I'm all prayed out for you, JT. Your whoring around has

destroyed me. I don't have time to go to God for your is-
sues because I'm too busy asking him to restore my soul."

She tried to walk away, but he grabbed hold of her arm.
"I'm sorry, Sanni. You deserved a much better husband—I
should have treated you right. But, I need you to do this
for me."

Cold, daggered eyes shot through him as she pulled her
arm from his grasp and walked away. "Do you need me to
call a cab so you can go back to whomever you stayed
with last night?"

He stood up. "I'm staying at the Marriott, Sanni. I
promise you that I didn't go to another woman last night.
Nor do I intend to do such a thing ever again."

"And we all know that you keep your promises, right
JT?"

He closed his eyes and rubbed his temples. When he
looked at her again he could see the resolve etched on her
face. He was ready to make a change, *but how does that
saying go?* he thought. *Too little, too late.* "What do I have
to do to prove to you that I'm for real?" JT asked.

She didn't answer him, just said, "Let me get the telephone book so you can look up the number for the cab
company."

"I don't need a cab. I'll just use your car."

Shaking her head, Cassandra told him, "Aaron has a
doctor's appointment tomorrow."

"What time?"

"Why?"

Impatiently, he demanded, "What time is his appointment, Sanni?"

"Three o'clock."

"Okay, well then I'll leave church at about one or two
and have the car back to you in time for baby boy's appointment."

Still shaking her head she told him, "Uh-uh, you're not

using my car, JT. It's as simple as that. Call up the woman who slashed your tires and have her come pick you up."

He ignored the last bit of her sentence and narrowed in on the part he knew he could object to. "Your car? Well, who pays the note on that car?"

"I do," she spat back. "I pay that note every time you lie, cheat, and humiliate me. I've paid that note with my broken heart."

"I never thought I'd see the day when you would be as bitter as your mother."

Before she could stop herself, she lifted her hand and smacked him in the face. Then she said, "I also have an appointment with a divorce attorney in the morning."

He rubbed his face. "Are you crazy? I'm not giving you a divorce."

With the sista-sista neck roll she said, "Be that as it may, I'm still going to see this attorney in the morning. You can sign the papers or don't; but now you know where I stand."

JT stepped back. Shaking his head, he picked up his keys from the kitchen counter and told her, "You're not going to any divorce attorney, I'm taking the car, Sanni. I'll be back before Aaron's appointment." He walked to the car in total bewilderment. Divorce! He was living through a nightmare that he prayed he would soon wake up from. He knew he had done Sanni wrong, but she was taking it to another level. What had gotten into her?

Jimmy called JT's cell phone while he was eating a TV dinner. "How did you get my cell number?" JT asked once he discovered who his caller was.

Jimmy snorted. "Are you kidding me? This is the information age, Bubba. Get use to it."

Rolling his eyes, JT demanded, "Don't call me again."

"See, that's your problem, JT. You've never understood the rules of the game. Well, let me school you." He coughed, then continued. "See, the man holding all the cards gets to call the shots."

What will it take to get rid of this loser? Fifteen years and no communication. Now Jimmy was staying in touch everyday like they were best friends or something. Sneering into the telephone, JT asked, "What do you want?"

"Maybe I want to go to your house and have a visit with your pretty little wife. What do you think of that?"

JT's grip tightened around the phone. His wife had put him out. He wasn't at his home to protect his family from maggots like Jimmy Littleton. So he had to sell some pretty big wolf tickets to insure his family's safety. JT put more bass in his voice as he said, "My family has nothing to do with this. Your beef is with me. But I swear to you, Jimmy, if you come to my house, I will shoot you."

Jimmy laughed. "Would you have to put down your Bible to pick up that gun, or are hypocrites like you allowed to hold your gun and Bible at the same time?"

JT didn't respond.

Jimmy continued. "Look, man. No sense getting upset. You wouldn't be at your house if I stopped by anyway. That sweet little wife of yours threw your sorry self out last night. I watched you leave. I would have paid her a visit, but the police showed up."

"Stay away from my family, do you hear me?"

Jimmy continued to taunt JT as he said, "Look at you. Getting all defensive over a woman you could care less about. The scuttlebutt says you only married her so her godfather would give you that congregation you got."

JT told him, "Well, your scuttlebutt is wrong. I love my wife."

"Yeah, that's usually the reason most men cheat. 'Cause they're so in love with their wives."

JT slammed down the phone. After everything else, he didn't have the energy to listen to a lecture from Jimmy Littleton. He laid his head down on his pillow and prepared for another sleepless night. Life had been so simple when God had been on his side.

CHAPTER 11

When JT got to the church, he called his mechanic to see when he would be able to pick up his car, and received a bit of happy news. His car would be ready by noon. Now if he could get his sermon done, he'd at least be able to deliver a clear and concise message on Sunday.

Before JT sat down at his desk, he noticed an envelope in his chair. He picked up the envelope and sat down. The flap was unsealed, so JT pulled a note out of the envelope and read it:

> JT,
>   I enjoyed every moment we spent together. I need you to know that I'm not willing to let you go. I don't know what it will take to convince you that we belong together. Does harm have to come to your family? I hope not.
>   Please make the right decision. We love each other and deserve to be together.

The letter wasn't signed, but JT thought Vivian had left it on his chair though he couldn't prove it. Diane also attended Faith Outreach, and, truth be told, he'd messed around with a few other members. Therefore, some woman was threatening his family, and he couldn't even call the cops on her because he couldn't prove which one of his former partners in dalliance had sent the letter.

He tore up the note and threw it in his trash. Rubbing his temples, he decided to just forget about it and get to work on his sermon. JT opened his Bible, and tried to get back to business. Nothing he read stuck to him. He couldn't find a message to preach. He bent his head and prayed for God to guide him, but God just ignored his pleas.

He started scribbling on his notepad just as Carl and Deke, his faithful deacons, walked into his office. "What's up, fellows?"

"Nothing much, Pastor. Just trying to finalize some details for Sunday's TV program," Carl told him.

The TV program. Now he had something else to worry about. Not only did he have to put a decent message together for his congregation while all this mess was going on in his life, but he also had to be wonderful in front of that camera.

Come to think of it, JT was sure that Jimmy had found him because of that rotten TV program. He'd only been on air once, and boom—his past had shown up. "Look, fellows, I'm thinking about canceling our airtime. I'm just not sure that we can afford it."

"We can't afford to cancel the program, Pastor. We've already borrowed more than a million dollars from the bank to get the equipment and pay for airtime. If we pull out now, we'll lose everything." Deke was the church accountant. He knew to the penny how much had been spent, and on what, but didn't feel the need to bore them with the weeds.

"That's right, Pastor," Carl agreed. "If you're not on air selling your tapes—oh, and did I mention that you need to write a couple books?"

"Yes, Carl, you've mentioned that," JT said.

"Well," Carl continued, "you need to be on air selling that stuff so we can recoup the money and pay off our bank loan."

"And as you know," Deke began, "with the current economic crisis America is dealing with, we are not about to get any extra money from the congregation to pay off this loan. We used the church building as collateral, so unless you want to see a foreclosure sign in this front yard, I suggest you get back on TV."

They were right. He didn't have time for chaos. As pastor of this church, he had a duty to see it back to financial health. "All right. You've made your point. Now let me get back to my sermon, or else no one will want to buy any of my other ministry tapes. So can I get back to my sermon now?"

Carl held up the notepad and files that were in his hand. "We really need to go over this information before Sunday."

"I trust you and Deke to make the decision. Whatever you want me to do, just tell me and I'll make it happen."

"There's something else, Pastor," Deke said with an embarrassed look on his face. He handed JT a fax and said, "You've been added to the list of pastors under investigation for inappropriate use of donor funds."

"What?" JT exploded as he stood and slammed his fist on his desk. "Why are they investigating me? The preachers on their first list all had jets. Do I have a jet? Am I flying people from state to state just for the heck of it?"

Preachers all over the nation were well aware that the United States Senate was on a crusade to prove that churches did not need to have tax exempt status. They planned to prove this by highlighting the fabulous life-styles of pastors and bishops. Members of the Senate cited private jets and golden toilets owned by tax exempt pastors with million-dollar salaries, and deduced that somebody must have their hand in the collection plate.

Deke said, "No, Pastor, you don't have a jet, but you do own a Bentley and a mansion."

"I don't own a mansion." JT's face twisted in anger as he exploded. "Compared to some of those other preacher's homes, I live in a shack."

Deke hunched his shoulders and lifted his hands. "I didn't send the letter, Pastor. But we do need to decide how we are going to respond to it."

"What do they want from us?"

"They want to see all of our financial records for the campaign drive we did to start the TV program. They want to make sure that all those funds went where we said they would be going," Deke responded

JT walked over to the window and watched the traffic go by. This was it for him. His church members might for-give him for getting a divorce if he played it the right way; but once they heard that he was also being investigated for taking donor money, they would stop paying their tithes, and transfer membership quicker than he could say Jim Baker.

"And what if they didn't?" Carl asked.

"I don't know what they will do. The Senate does not have the authority to make us turn over our records. They're just asking that we comply with their wishes," Deke said.

JT asked, "What if we don't comply?"

"Again," Deke said, "I don't know what the ramifica-tions of not complying are. If we didn't spend the money as we said it would be spent, we might lose our tax exempt status, or in a very extreme case, I guess somebody could go to prison."

And on that happy note, JT turned back around to face his deacons. "I need to be alone for a little while, gentlemen. Let me think this over."

"All right, Pastor," Deke said.

"Yeah, we can talk about this stuff later. You worry about your sermon for right now," Carl added as he and Deke left the office.

JT sat back down at his desk. He looked at his Bible, notepad, files, and notes that waited in his in-basket for him to review; he was sick of it all. In one swoop of his arm, he knocked everything off his desk, then leaned back in his chair and closed his eyes.

The phone rang. JT almost didn't answer it. He wanted peace and quiet. There were times when he would sit in one spot for hours waiting for an answer from God. Today, JT just wanted to sit in this spot and be numb. But he could sit there until the rapture came and nothing would change for him, so he picked up the phone and said, "This is Pastor JT Thomas."

"I know what I want."

"Who is this?" JT asked.

"Don't play dumb. You know who you're talking to."

Rolling his eyes, JT said, "Look, Jimmy, I don't have time to play games with you today."

"Oh, you don't have to play. I'll just call up your local TV news station and that gospel station you air your little Bible thumping sermons on and tell them everything I know about the illustrious Pastor JT Thomas."

"What do you want, Jimmy?"

"Naw, that's all right. You ain't got to humor me. You're too big and important to have time for little ol' three strikes Jimmy. I'll just find my way down to the news station."

"Just tell me what you want. You said you know, so tell me."

"That's better," Jimmy told him. "You sound scared enough to do what I tell you."

"You're wasting my time, just tell me what you want," JT demanded.

"Meet me for lunch and I'll lay my plans out for you. At Major Hoople's in the Flats. Do you know where that is?"

"At the corner of Riverbed and Columbus Roads?"

"Yeah," Jimmy responded, then asked, "It's not too common for your elite taste is it?"

Ignoring the jab, JT said, "I know the place. I can be there in about twenty minutes."

They hung up and JT grabbed his keys and headed out. When he got to the parking lot and found his car missing, he started to panic until he remembered that he'd driven Cassandra's car. Opening his cell phone he dialed his wife. "Did you take the car?" he asked as soon as she was on the line.

"Sure did. My bitter mother brought me over there to get it. I have a set of keys to *my* car too, you know."

His shoulders slumped. "I told you I would bring the car home in time for Aaron's appointment."

"Yeah right, after you drove some of your temple sluts around in my Lexus. That ain't happening. You can catch a cab until your car gets fixed."

She hung up and he slammed his phone shut. "Dawg, that woman don't care nothing about me." And the knowledge of that stung.

He went back into his office and called a cab. It was twenty minutes before the cab picked him up and dropped him off at his house. He knew he was being petty, but he got into Cassandra's car and backed out of the driveway anyway.

Cassandra ran out of the house screaming at him. JT

rolled down the window and said, "I'll be back before Aaron's appointment." He then pulled off.

Taking the time to go home and get Cassandra's car cost him thirty minutes. Needless to say, during the whole ride over to the restaurant JT imagined that Jimmy had gotten tired of waiting on him, left the restaurant, and was now giving his story to *Hard Copy*, *Star* or some other rag dedicated to selling other people's sorrows.

But to his relief (or regret), Jimmy was still waiting on him. "You're late," he snapped as JT approached the booth.

"Relax. I had car problems."

"Oh yeah, that's right. Your car is in the shop."

JT stopped walking and pointed at him. "It was you."

"Me? What?"

"You know what—you slashed my tires."

Jimmy laughed. "Boy, it sounds to me like you don' made some woman mad. How many of them chicken-heads you sleeping with at that church?"

JT slid into their booth without responding.

"Do you think you could hook me up with one of 'em?" Jimmy grinned at JT, showing off his rotten front tooth.

JT lifted the menu and studied it with interest.

"Come on, man, why you gotta be so stingy? You got that pretty woman at home. Why can't—"

JT put his menu down. "Leave my wife out of this."

"Now which wife would that be?"

JT was silent. He really didn't want to go there. Jimmy knew him from back in the day. He had all the dirt on him. All the dirt that JT prayed would never be unearthed.

"Relax man, your secrets are safe with me," Jimmy assured him.

"At what price?"

"Don't we just get straight to the point?" Jimmy asked with a smirk on his face.

The waitress came to the table and took JT's order. Jimmy already had a turkey sandwich in front of him. "I'll just have a glass of water for now," JT said.

"Coming right up," she told him as she put her pad and pencil back in her apron and walked off.

When she left, Jimmy turned back to JT. "Hey, remember Fat Roy. He was the enforcer at the last house we tried to rob that night."

"You said you knew what you wanted. Tell me and let me get out of here."

"You don't want to know what happened to Fat Roy?" Jimmy asked while picking his teeth.

JT rolled his eyes. "What do you want, Jimmy? I have things to do."

"All right," Jimmy said as he leaned back in his seat. "I want the two hundred and fifty thousand you owe me."

"What? Man, you must be crazy. I don't owe you two hundred and fifty thousand."

Jimmy held up his hands as if to say he didn't want to start a fight. "Look, JT, I know we were supposed to split the money we stole, but the way I see it, you had the benefit of holding onto that money for fifteen years. You could have invested it and tripled our money by now for all I know."

"Well, I didn't," JT said.

The waitress dropped off JT's water.

When she walked away, Jimmy said, "Too bad for you, because I need my money. I'm trying to get out of this country so I can stay out of prison. So I'm going to need my money."

"Look, I'm going to be honest with you. I held onto your money for many years. But after Lester got killed, I went back to New Orleans to ask Mona for a divorce."

Jimmy raised his hand and said, "Spare me the history lesson. I already know Lester got himself shot up."

"What I'm trying to tell you," JT continued, "is that Mona refused to give me a divorce unless I gave her a bunch of money. All I had left was the money I was saving for you. I really needed that divorce, so I gave it to her."

"What!" Jimmy exploded.

"Calm down, Jimmy. It's not as if we worked for the money. It was one night of looting in which we made two hundred and fifty thousand dollars. And I gave Mona a hundred and twenty five thousand ."

With nostrils flaring, Jimmy asked, "Do you really expect me to believe that you just handed over that kind of money to Mona?"

"Believe what you want, but that's what happened."

Jimmy's eyes were filled with hatred as his fist clenched. "I'm not sure you understand me, Pastor. Give me my money or you will not live long enough to regret it."

JT leaned in closer to Jimmy and said, "It doesn't matter how much you threaten me, Jimmy. I don't have the money and I don't know how you expect me to get it."

"I don't care if you take it out of the collection plate. Just get me my money."

JT stood up. "I can't do that."

Jimmy grabbed JT's arm and jerked him around so that they were face-to-face when he said, "Play me if you want, JT. But I will bury you."

JT snatched his arm away from Jimmy and walked out of the restaurant as all that he had built crumbled down around him. He had done a lot of wrong in his life, but he hadn't done what those senators were accusing him of. His house was mortgaged to the hilt and he'd paid for his Bentley with his own money—It might have come from the money that he and Jimmy had stolen, but it sure didn't come from his hand being in the church collection plate, and it never would.

He walked out to his wife's car and sat there for a moment. His head was spinning. Thoughts of running away and starting a new life flooded his mind. He'd gotten away with it for fifteen years, whose to say he couldn't just reinvent himself again? He put the key in the ignition, and shifted the car to reverse so he could back out of the parking lot. Someone knocked on his window. He put the car back in park and rolled down the window. A police officer stood in front of him, looking as if he had just caught a criminal red-handed. *What now?* JT thought.

The police officer said, "Out of the car, mister."

"Excuse me?" JT responded.

"Out of the car," the police officer said again. "You're driving a stolen car."

"No I'm not. This is my wife's car. Mine is in the shop, so I'm using hers."

"Let me see your ID, sir," the police officer said.

JT handed over his driver's license, then was informed that he would have to wait in the back of the police car while the officer checked out his statement. While sitting there, JT remembered that Cassandra's car was registered in her mother's name. When they purchased the car two years ago, it was supposed to be a Mother's Day present for Mattie Daniels, but the old hag hadn't wanted the car. She said it was too fancy for her. So Cassandra decided keep it herself, but they never bothered with the registration. Now JT knew why the car had been reported stolen. Mattie would love to see him in jail.

The police officer turned to him with a sympathetic look on his face. "Sir, I'm sorry but the lady who owns this car says that you stole it from her daughter."

"Her daughter is my wife. And I paid for that car myself. That mean, old woman never even wanted the car," JT said.

"I'm going through a divorce myself, Mr. Thomas—"

"Who says I'm getting a divorce?" JT demanded.

"That's what your mother-in-law told the police when she reported the car stolen. Sorry, sir, but I have to take you in."

As they drove past the entrance of the restaurant, JT could see Jimmy staring at him; gloating, because he was finally seeing his old friend being carted away in a police car, as he had been the day JT watched but did nothing to help.

CHAPTER 12

While JT sat in his jail cell waiting for his secretary to bail him out, he wondered how things had gotten so bad. Being honest, JT admitted that things had gone south before he'd started sleeping around, and before he'd stopped reading the Bible as a diligent steward of the Word. Things had gone bad for him when Cassandra had lost their first baby. She had been a beautiful little girl. But JT never even had a chance to hear her cry; never saw the sparkle in her brown eyes. Their baby had died shortly after Cassandra delivered her. That was the saddest day of his life. And although JT hated to admit it; that was the day he'd stopped completely trusting God.

"Why did you let her die?" JT asked as he looked heavenward. "Didn't You know that I wasn't strong enough to deal with something like that?"

JT stood up and walked the length of his cell. He walked back and forth trying to think this thing through. Yes, JT reasoned, God did know all. So He must have known that JT would fall after the death of his daughter.

"Is that why You waited years before giving up on me? Were You giving me time to come back to You? Did you know that I was angry with You all this time?"

JT lay down on his cot as his mind's eye went back to that awful day; the day he stopped believing.

"Push, Sanni!" JT said, standing next to her in the delivery room.

"I'm trying. It hurts," she cried.

She had been in labor for twelve hours, and had been in active push mode for the last thirty minutes. The labor went smoothly. They sat in the room joking and playing games. But when the actual delivery began, the pain became too much for Cassandra. She pushed and pushed but nothing happened.

The labor and delivery nurse gently touched Cassandra's arm and said, "I see the head, so rest for a minute. But as soon as you feel the next contraction, push with all your strength."

JT squeezed her hand. "You can do it, honey. Our Sarah is almost here."

The monitor on the right side of Cassandra's bed started beeping. Dr. Monroe looked up, and JT saw the concern on his face. "What? What's wrong?" JT asked.

Dr. Monroe turned to his nurse and said, "We may need to do a C-section. I need you to get the room set up for that, just in case."

The monitor was still beeping. Cassandra clung to JT. Fear was in her voice as she asked, "What's going on?"

JT turned back to Dr. Monroe. "Tell us, man. What's wrong."

"The baby's heart rate is weakening. If we can't get the baby out with the next push, we're going to do a C-section."

Everything happened so fast after that, JT barely had a chance to catch his breath or pray. Cassandra felt an-

other contraction. She pushed and pushed until Dr. Monroe told them he was holding the baby's head. Cassandra laid back thinking her job was over.

Dr. Monroe hollered, "Push one more time, Cassandra. We need to get the rest of the body out."

Cassandra sat back up and pushed again.

"That's it, Sanni. She's out now," JT told her as he saw his baby slide out of Cassandra's body. The whole process was a true mystery to JT. It was pretty amazing how God was able to put life into another human being.

Dr. Monroe cut the umbilical cord, and handed the baby to the nurse.

"It's a girl!" the nurse said as she took the baby to the opposite side of the room to clean her up.

Cassandra smiled. "I told you we were having a girl."

"You were right. I'm sure she is as beautiful as her mother," JT said, wiping the sweat from Cassandra's face and neck.

"I want to see my baby. Go get her, JT," Cassandra said as she yawned. Her eyelids started to close.

"Let them finish cleaning Sarah. They'll bring her over to us."

With another yawn, Cassandra asked, "Why isn't she crying?"

At that moment JT turned to look at the baby. Dr. Monroe was standing in front of her. He looked at JT. JT saw the distress on the man's face and knew the answer before he asked, "Why isn't she crying?"

"Why, Lord, why did you allow my child to be born with such a weak heart that she couldn't make it through the delivery? Why didn't you just fix her heart?"

Before JT could get an answer to his query, his cell was opened and the deputy told him, "You've been bailed out. Let's go."

He followed the policeman as he directed him to where Betty was waiting for him.

"Thanks for coming to get me, Betty. I appreciate it." JT said.

"It's not a problem, Pastor. I just don't understand why you would get arrested for driving your wife's car," she said as they walked toward the door.

No way was he going to tell his secretary that his wife threw him out. "It's just a big misunderstanding. The car is in her mother's name. Mattie called it in stolen, but Cassandra and I will get to the bottom of this."

Betty looked a little confused, but said, "I sure hope so, Pastor."

JT had her drop him at the car dealership so he could pick up his car. He then called Cassandra and said, "Do you know that your mother had me arrested?"

Cassandra hung up on him.

"No she didn't," JT said as he dialed her back again.

This time when Cassandra answered, she said, "Stop calling me, JT, or I'm going to get a restraining order against you."

"What? A restraining order against me? I'm your husband, Cassandra. Or have you forgotten that?"

"I didn't forget. You're the one who conveniently forgot about me every time you wanted to have sex with another woman. Now please leave me alone." She hung up again.

JT would have called her a third time, but he knew it wouldn't do any good. He needed to get back to church anyway. They had Bible study tonight and he hadn't even decided what he would preach. When he arrived back at church, he went into his office and opened his file cabinet. He searched through his numerous messages and came across one titled, "Don't Sweat the Small Stuff." Every pastor JT knew had a "Don't Sweat the Small Stuff" message in his file cabinet. *And why was that?* JT asked himself. *Because they worked.*

He sat down at his desk, went over his message, and reviewed the scriptures that related to his message. By the time people started arriving at church that evening, JT felt confident enough to deliver his message. He grabbed his Bible and his notes, and got up to go to his pulpit.

The door to his office burst open and Deacon Benson stood there with nostrils flaring. "You been sleeping with my wife," Deacon Benson declared, loud enough for the entire church to hear.

JT tried to calm him. "Benson, I don't know what Diane has been telling you, but she's lying."

"Oh, she's lying, huh?" Deacon Benson moved away from the door, advancing on JT. "What about my baby girl? Diane says belongs to you!"

JT stood behind his desk, trying to determine if he should make a run for the office door, or if he should shut himself inside his closet and try to hold the door shut. Deacon Benson was built like George Foreman, big and tall. He was several inches taller than JT. "That's your baby, Deacon. Don't believe that woman. I don't know why she's saying this stuff."

"I'll tell you why she's saying it," Deacon Benson said, now in front of JT's desk. "Because you slept with her, you jerk." Deacon Benson reached out, trying to grab JT.

JT jumped back, dropped his Bible, and ran out of his office. But Deacon Benson was right behind him. He grabbed JT by the collar, turned him around, and punched him in the face.

"You are going to pay for what you did to my family," Benson said as he hit JT in the face again.

JT fell on the ground and hurriedly tried to get back up.

Elder Unders and Deacon Carl ran up the hall and pulled Deacon Benson away from JT. Elder Unders said,

"What's wrong with you, Deacon? You know better than to touch God's elect."

"God didn't call that man. He's evil," Deacon Benson said as he squirmed under the hold of his captors.

"Do you want me to call the police, Pastor?" Deacon Carl asked.

JT took the handkerchief from his pocket and wiped blood from his mouth. "No, don't call the police. Benson and I just had a misunderstanding. Isn't that right, Benson?"

Benson pulled his arms away from Elder Unders and Carl, and said, "Yeah, I guess I just don't understand how a man could claim to love God and sleep around with other men's wives." Benson walked away from the group, vowing never to return to Faith Outreach again.

Some of the members had come out of the sanctuary to see what was going on in the hall. Elder Unders told them, "Go on back into the sanctuary. There's nothing to see out here." He turned back to JT and asked, "Are you okay?"

"Yeah," JT told him, still wiping his lip. "But do you mind delivering the message tonight? I need to get out of here for a little while."

"I'll take care of it, Pastor. Don't worry about the service tonight," Elder Unders said.

"Are you sure you don't want to call the police?" Deacon Carl asked.

JT waved him off as he went back to his office, got his keys, and walked out of the building.

When he got to his car there was a note on the windshield. He pulled it off and read: *I want my money. Don't make me hurt you.*

JT was angry now. He was tired of being bullied. He ripped the note into multiple pieces, balled it up and threw it in the outdoor trash bin.

* * *

Jimmy Littleton sat outside the church. He had followed JT from the police station, to the car dealership, and then to church. Now he watched JT disrespect him by ripping his note up and throwing it in the trash. That was it as far as Jimmy was concerned. He was fuming as he watched JT jump in his Bentley and leave the church. Jimmy wanted his money back and had tried to make a deal with JT to get it. But did JT take his offer seriously? No. JT had given his money to Mona. Jimmy pounded his fist against the steering wheel in the Toyota Camry he'd stolen earlier in the day. He used to steal SUVs, but with the price of gas, he'd had to scale down.

Sometimes, Jimmy wondered if he needed therapy. He had only been out of prison a couple of months, and there was already a warrant out for his arrest because of the convenience store he'd robbed before leaving New Orleans. And now he was stealing cars, waiting outside a church, stalking a preacher.

"Get a hold of yourself, man," Jimmy said. Yes, he was a thief; but he'd never menacingly stalked anybody. He'd also never hated anybody as much as he hated JT Thomas. As he followed JT all the way to the Marriott, his hatred kept growing as he thought about how he'd lived in poverty all this time, while JT had become the king of the jungle. So, Jimmy felt the pressure his foot put on the pedal. He wanted to stop himself, but as JT stepped into the parking lot, Jimmy thought of vengeance and his foot slammed down.

JT drove down the street wondering how things had gone so wrong so fast. He wanted to go home and talk to Cassandra, but she had thrown him out. Why was God doing this to him? He wasn't that bad. JT knew plenty of pastors who were much worse than he was, and yet they continued to flourish.

And what was JT doing? He was headed to the Marriott hotel alone, to eat a TV dinner and stare at the walls. He didn't even know if he would have a church to go back to once word got around of what Deacon Benson did and why he did it. As he pulled into the Marriott parking lot, JT was tempted to pull back out and go home so he could talk to Cassandra. But then he remembered Cassandra's threat of a restraining order.

He got out of the car and stood there for a moment with his hands in his pocket. He was confused. Didn't know what to do or which way to go. A lot had happened to him in the week since God had tired of his trifflin' behavior and given up on him. He had sunk real low. *What am I going to do, Lord*, he silently prayed. His lips were not moving but his heart was pouring out to God as he walked through the parking lot, headed for the entry door. "My wife hates me. I'm about to lose my church, and my old friend Jimmy wants to steal money from the church."

He was so intent with his one-way conversation, that he didn't see the car speeding up until it was upon him. JT faced the car and saw Jimmy behind the wheel, right before it slammed into him so hard that he did three somersaults into the air. His body then landed with a thud in the middle of the street. As the wind was knocked out of him and just before darkness overtook him, JT heard himself whisper, "Help me, Lord."

CHAPTER 13

Cassandra rushed to the hospital the moment she had been informed of JT's accident. JT was in surgery, so Cassandra was filling out the consent form as her mother arrived at the hospital to pick up her sons.

"How are you doing, sweetie?" Mattie asked as she gave Cassandra a hug.

Cassandra's hands shook as she tried to fill out the forms. She put the pen down and said, "I don't know, Mom. They say he's banged up pretty bad."

Mattie sat down next to her daughter. "I'm sorry to hear that."

Cassandra wondered if her mother was truly sorry. She hated everything about JT, so if he died, Cassandra imagined that her mother would dance on his casket. But then she thought that was too mean, even for her mother. So she decided to take her mother at her word. "We'll know more when he comes out of surgery," Cassandra said, then picked up the papers to finish filling them out.

"Where are the boys?" Mattie asked Cassandra.

"JT's secretary, Betty Marks, took them to the cafeteria.

She should have them back here in a few minutes." Cassandra's voice shook as she became overwhelmed by the thought that her boys might never see their father alive again. She put her head on her mother's shoulder and cried, "He was run over outside of the Marriott. This wouldn't have happened if I hadn't put him out."

"Oh, no you don't," Mattie said as she lifted Cassandra's head off her shoulder and looked her in the face. "Don't you dare blame yourself. That man has treated you horribly. You had every right to throw him out. You should have done it sooner."

Cassandra wiped the tears from her face. "Don't start, Mom."

"I'm not starting nothing. I'm just saying don't blame yourself."

Cassandra opened her mouth to say something, but then noticed a nurse walking toward them. The woman wore a smock with SpongeBob SquarePants on it, and looked to be in a rush. Cassandra stood up. "Did something happen to JT?"

The nurse shook her head. "No, ma'am. He's still in surgery. I just need the forms back. Are you done filling them out?"

"Oh, yes," Cassandra said as she bent to pick the papers up. She signed the document on top and handed the papers to the woman. "How much longer before we will know something?"

"The doctor should be out within the hour."

"Thank you," Cassandra said.

The nurse walked away. But as Cassandra was getting ready to sit back down next to her mother, she saw Diane Benson running down the hall toward her. However, instead of coming over to Cassandra, Diane stopped the nurse. Cassandra heard her ask, "How is JT? Can I see him? I really need to see him."

Mattie harrumphed as she stood and marched toward Diane and the nurse. Mattie wagged her finger as she said, "Now you listen here, Diane Benson, you are not going to start no mess in this hospital. I know all about women like you, and I'm prepared to deal with you."

There were tears in Diane's eyes as she turned toward Mattie. "What am I starting, Ms. Mattie?" Diane lifted her arm and pointed at Cassandra. "She threw him out. I'm just here to make sure he knows that somebody in this world cares about what happens to him."

"He's got a wife who cares. The rest is none of your business," Mattie told Diane.

The nurse lifted her hands. "Look, I've got to get back to work." She turned to Diane and said, "You'll have to ask Mrs. Thomas about her husband."

Defiantly, Diane said, "I don't have to ask her anything."

The nurse shook her head as she walked away.

Mattie walked away from Diane. Her voice was raised as she asked Cassandra, "You just gon' let this woman walk in here and demand to see your husband?"

Cassandra actually wanted to thank Diane for showing up when she did. She had almost forgot that she and JT were through. She was tired of all the drama surrounding her husband. She sat down and told her mother, "Let her stay, let her go, I just don't care about JT's flings anymore."

"See, I told you she didn't care," Diane said as she flopped into a seat on the opposite side of the room.

Even though Cassandra had decided that she didn't care, she was determined that Diane would sit in that seat for a decade before she would allow her to see JT. Many other members of the church arrived. JT came out of the surgery and the doctor told Cassandra that she could go in to see him, but she didn't want to do that.

JT had now been out of surgery for two days; but she

had still not gone into her husband's room. Instead, she allowed some of the church members—but not Diane—to go in to check on their pastor while she sat, reading a book and waiting. But what was she waiting for? Was she scared to see JT all bruised and battered as his doctor had reported, or was it that she was just so sick of JT and all his lies that she just couldn't endure one more lie from him? She wanted to know about the accident, but she didn't want to ask JT because she no longer believed a word that came out of his mouth.

"Cassandra."

She heard the voice and knew immediately that it was Bishop Turner. Cassandra put down the novel that she was reading, stood up, walked over to her godfather, and hugged him. "I knew you would come," she whispered as he held her tight.

"I'm so sorry this happened. How is he doing, honey?"

Cassandra moved out of her godfather's embrace and sat back down. "The doctor says he's in a lot of pain and really banged up."

"Is he asleep now? How did he look the last time you were in there with him?" Bishop asked Cassandra.

"I haven't been in there yet," she told him.

He looked at his watch and then asked, "You haven't been in to see him today?"

"I haven't gone into his room since he arrived at the hospital," she admitted with her eyes downcast.

Bishop Turner sighed as he took off his hat and sat down next to Cassandra. He put his arm around her shoulder and gently squeezed. "I know things haven't been that great between you and JT lately, but do you think you should be sitting out here rather than tending to your husband?"

"You know what I really think, Bishop?" Cassandra said as tears spilled down her face. "I think his girlfriends should have to tend to him. Two of them had the nerve to come out to the hospital to see him, but do you think they stayed or even offered to nurse him through his recuperation process? No. So, I guess that's my job—mending this no good dog so he can get well enough to flaunt his women in my face again."

Rubbing and squeezing Cassandra's shoulder, Bishop said, "I know that you're not in a good place with your marriage right now. Sometimes we men can be very imperfect people. My wife would tell you the same thing about me."

Cassandra shook her head. "Not you, Bishop. You would never treat your wife the way JT has treated me."

Sorrow filled his eyes as he admitted, "I've made my mistakes too, honey. Susan forgave me and we've made a good life together since then." The look of horror on Cassandra's face was as if someone had knocked her idol down right in front of her. "I'm sorry if that shocks you, but sometimes we pastors get big heads and forget that the people adoring our ministry actually belong to God and not us. When that happens, a pastor will fall just as easily as a new babe in Christ."

"I don't know if I can do what your wife did, Bishop. I'm just tired of it all."

Bishop stood up, reached for Cassandra's hand, and then pulled her up with him. "Why don't we take it a day at a time? Let's go see your husband. Okay, sweetie?"

Cassandra let go of Bishop's hand and walked toward her husband's room. She hesitated for a moment at the door. She was still angry about the confrontation she had with JT's mistress, who had the nerve to be upset when the nurses wouldn't let her in because she wasn't family. Cassandra shook off the memory and opened the door to her husband's room. JT lay in the bed, looking at her with pain-filled eyes. His left arm was bandaged from shoulder to wrist, and his right arm and leg were both in slings. His face no longer reminded her of the warm caramel that coated delicious red apples at summer fairs. It was swollen two sizes bigger than normal and black-and-blue. Tubes were everywhere; two were in JT's mouth.

She turned away from him, wanting to run, but Bishop was in the doorway to halt her exit. He grabbed her and hugged her. "It's okay, honey. He's battered and bruised, but the man you fell in love with is still there."

That's the problem, Cassandra thought. The man she fell in love with had become the man she now despised, and she didn't know if she had enough God in her to help her husband through this difficult time. "I don't want to look at him," Cassandra cried as she leaned into Bishop's chest.

"Monster."

Bishop Turner and Cassandra both heard JT say something, but it was so mumbled because of the tubes in his mouth that they couldn't understand it. Bishop moved Cassandra closer to JT's bed and asked him, "What did you say, son?"

"I'm a monster."

Cassandra understood him that time, and she agreed. JT looked like a monster. But what he said next confused her.

"God's work."

CHAPTER 14

A young police officer came to the hospital to see JT, but JT couldn't answer the man's questions. He couldn't even write down his answers, since one arm was in a cast and the other in a sling. The officer said he would come back when JT could speak. The next day, Vivian Sampson came to visit. JT watched her walk in with a smug smile on her face. She had a basket of yellow and white flowers in her hand. She stood over his bed and asked, "Where do I put these?"

Words were still coming out like a mumble for JT, and he couldn't point, either.

"Oh, you poor thing. I heard that you were having a hard time communicating," Vivian said as she walked over to an empty table and set the flowers on it. She turned around, leaned against the table, and said, "You really look bad. When do you suppose the swelling will go down on your head?" She put her hand over her mouth to stifle a giggle as she walked back to his bed. "I'm sorry. I keep forgetting that you can't talk."

JT knew that Vivian was still mad at him for breaking it

off with her. He also knew that he couldn't defend himself against Vivian if she decided to do something to him, so he prayed that a nurse or somebody would come into his room before this sociopath smothered him with his own pillow.

Vivian put her hands on the sling that held JT's right arm. His eyes implored her not to hurt him. But Vivian obviously couldn't read eye language because she began to shake the sling. JT's eyes watered as a scream of agony escaped his mouth.

Vivian let go of the sling and moved away from the bed as a nurse with fire red hair ran into the room. "What's going on in here?"

"He's in a lot of pain, poor thing," Vivian said as she moved back toward JT's bed.

JT mumbled his response, but no one understood. The nurse walked over to him and asked, "What's wrong, Mr. Thomas?"

JT's eyes flashed fear as he looked from Vivian and then back to his nurse. The nurse looked at JT's visitor and asked, "Are you a member of the family?"

"I attend the church he pastors."

"I'm not sure you're supposed to be in here. His wife has requested that he have no visitors right now."

"I don't think JT has a problem with me being in here," Vivian told the nurse defiantly.

Fear lingered in JT's eyes when the nurse looked back at him for confirmation. She told Vivian, "Why don't you leave your name at the nurse's station and we will clear you with Mrs. Thomas." The nurse grabbed Vivian's arm and said, "Let me show you where the station is."

Vivian snatched away from her. "I don't need your help. I can leave on my own, and I certainly don't need to leave my name at your nurse's station." Vivian strutted out of JT's room without looking back.

JT rested his head on his pillow and breathed a bit easier. But he would not rest for long. Two days after Vivian's visit, Deacon Benson came to see him. The deacon didn't come bearing flowers or a smug smile. He just sat down in the chair next to JT's bed with a Bible in his hand.

The tubes had been taken out of JT's mouth, and even though the areas around his lips were swollen, he was able to communicate a little better. The sling on his leg had also been removed. "Deacon," JT said as he watched the man sit down.

Deacon Benson looked at JT for a moment. There was a bitter sadness in his eyes as he said, "My wife left me today, Pastor. She said she couldn't continue living a lie."

JT wanted to say something, but he just didn't know what could make this situation better. He had called this man a friend and then slept with his wife, and now she had left him. JT hoped that Benson wasn't there to finish the job he'd started at the church. The call button was an inch away from his thumb, so he could get a nurse in there if he had to.

Deacon Benson put the Bible on his lap, opened it to Psalm 55 and began reading without looking at JT.

Give ear to my prayer, O God; and hide not thyself from my supplication. Attend unto me, and hear me: I mourn my complaint, and make a noise . . .

For it was not an enemy that reproached me; then I could have borne it: neither was it he that hated me that did magnify himself against me; then I would have hid myself from him: But it was you, a man mine equal, my guide, and mine friend.

When Deacon Benson finished reading, he closed his Bible and stood to leave.

JT had wronged this man by sleeping with his wife. JT's

right arm had been taken out of the sling earlier in the day. It still hurt, but he managed to lift it halfway as he said, "Wait."

JT's voice didn't sound much like mumbling anymore, so Deacon Benson understood him, but he didn't stop walking toward the door.

"I—I'm sorry," JT said, and what surprised him most was that he really meant it. He was truly sorry for the way he had messed up everyone's lives; he just didn't know how to fix it.

Deacon Benson hesitated at the door for a moment, and then, without looking back, he walked out of the room.

After that visit, JT was pretty much left alone. Cassandra hadn't visited him since the day she'd come in his room with Bishop Turner. The nurses told him that she called them several times a day to check on him, but he desperately needed to see her. Being left alone provided him too much time to think about the lives he had ruined.

Margie Milner was the first woman with whom JT had cheated on Cassandra. He had increasingly gotten bolder as his affair with Margie appeared to go undetected. He remembered how angry Margie had become when she discovered that JT had started seeing other women, and how she felt that he was cheating on her. He had mixed her mind up so badly that Margie didn't realize that what they had was nothing like a marriage. She didn't understand that God had joined him and Cassandra together; not him, Cassandra, and Margie. But looking back, JT couldn't blame Margie for all that had happened because of her misunderstanding.

Margie had been a deaconess at Faith Outreach for five years before JT became the pastor. She was faithful to the Lord and handled her responsibilities without complaint. One night, the two of them were in JT's office with the door closed. They were going over details for the church picnic when JT brushed his hand against hers. The first time was an accident, but he felt an electric charge that had been missing with him and Cassandra ever since they'd lost the baby. So, he put his hand back over Margie's, and let it rest there until she looked at him. At that moment he saw the hunger in her eyes; she was lonely too. She needed him to take away the loneliness from her heart and maybe, just maybe, she could restore joy to his soul. At least that's what he told himself as he leaned over and kissed Margie. Their affair lasted two years, until the day that Cassandra gave birth to Jerome, and demanded that he end his affair.

Margie had left Faith Outreach after JT ended their affair. The last JT heard, Margie had not joined another church. She was now unwed, but living with a guy, pregnant with his baby. JT had ruined Margie's life, but he had never even taken the time to mourn her fall from grace. He'd never cried for Margie, but as a dose of reality was poured onto his memories, a tear trickled down his face. And in the dark of night, when the hospital was mostly empty and quiet, JT wished that Jimmy would come into his room and finish him off. When that didn't happen, JT seriously thought about doing it himself.

Then the police came to see him. A white officer with dirty blond hair stood next to his bed with a notepad and pen in his hand. "I'm Officer Michael McDaniels and I've been assigned to your case. Did you get a look at the car or the driver?"

JT wasn't sure he wanted to talk to the police about this incident. But if he didn't, Jimmy might attack Cassandra or his children next. JT wouldn't be able to live with himself if that happened. "I don't remember the car, but that doesn't matter," JT said.

"Why do you think the car doesn't matter?"

"Because Jimmy steals cars all the time. I'm sure it wasn't his."

The officer looked up from his notepad. "Who's Jimmy?"

JT decided he'd tell McDaniels enough of the truth to help him investigate this crime. "Jimmy is an old high school friend of mine. He's been in and out of jail since we left high school, and he showed up at my church this week trying to extort money from me."

"Did you give him any money?"

JT shook his head. "No, he wanted me to steal it from my church. So, I told him I couldn't help him."

"Why would he come to you for money? Have you kept in touch with him since high school?"

"I hadn't seen him in fifteen years. The only thing I can think is that he was so desperate to get some money that he started reaching out to anyone he thought could give it to him. Maybe I was his last resort, maybe that's why he ran me over. But I can't say that for sure."

When Officer McDaniels left, JT laid his head on his pillow, wondering if he would eventually be arrested. Once the police found Jimmy and discovered that JT stole money from a drug dealer, what would happen? *Do people really get arrested for stealing from drug dealers?*

JT was in the hospital for two weeks. The swelling in his face had gone down, so he didn't look like the monster he had a few days ago. But that was on the outside. As far as Cassandra was concerned, JT was still a monster. She didn't like him, and didn't want to take him home; nor did she want to help him recuperate. But she found herself in a no-win situation. She had married this man for better or worse. So even though things were pretty bad for them, she couldn't desert him. That just wasn't who she was.

She walked over to his bed and tried to put a smile on her face, but the smile was lopsided. "How are you doing today?"

JT looked up at his wife. Although the swelling had gone down on his face, he still had black-and-blue bruising below his eyes, on his forehead, and right below his cheekbone. "I'm not doing too well," he told her.

"What's wrong? Are you in pain?"

He shook his head. "I'm too drugged up right now to feel much pain in my body. I was just lying here thinking about all the stupid things I've done in my life and how I've hurt and corrupted so many people."

Cassandra didn't want to get into a conversation about all the evil JT had done. If she continued to think about it, she might just leave him in this hospital to fend for himself. "The doctor says you will be released today. Are you excited about that?"

His eyes were moist as he responded. "I've hurt you so bad these last few years, I'm wondering if you would rather that I go to a nursing home, so I could have round-the-clock care and you wouldn't have to take time from the boys to help me recuperate?"

This was not the JT that Cassandra was used to. He had never cared how much extra work his thoughtless behavior cost her. She was just expected to go out of her way to please him.

A nurse walked in with JT's release papers in her hand. She looked at Cassandra with bright, playful eyes and asked, "I hope you're ready to take your husband home, because we are sure tired of waiting on him hand and foot."

Cassandra and JT looked at each other. The room was uncomfortably silent for a moment. That's when Cassandra saw the pain in her husband's eyes. Somehow she knew this pain she was witnessing was real, and she desperately wanted to know where it was coming from.

"Is something wrong?" the nurse asked, release papers still in her hand.

Cassandra turned away from her husband and took the papers from the nurse. "Nothing's wrong. We're just ready to go home, isn't that right, JT?" Cassandra said.

CHAPTER 15

For the first month that JT was home, he could barely move. A physical therapist worked with him four times a week. Slowly, JT began to recover. After two weeks of recovery, JT was given a cane to move around. But because of the excruciating pain he felt while walking, JT only used the cane to go to his adjoining bathroom and back to his bed. One day, while lying in bed thinking over his life and how far he had fallen, Bishop Turner came to see him.

Bishop sat down in the chair next to JT's bed and asked, "How are you feeling today?"

"Not so good, Bishop," JT said as he tried to sit up, but the pain of movement stopped him in his tracks. JT blew out hot air and fell back on his pillow. "I'll be much better when I'm free of pain."

"I know it's been tough for you. Cassandra doesn't look like she's getting much sleep. I'm worried about her also."

"You're always worried about Cassandra. But she's a grown woman, Bishop. She can take care of herself," JT said.

"Yeah, but I asked you to be her protector so she wouldn't have to take care of herself," Bishop said with noticeable sadness in his voice.

JT knew this visit wouldn't be friendly. "What do you want me to do, Bishop? I know I messed up. Cassandra hasn't forgiven me for anything. She barely let me come home to recuperate."

Anger was etched on Bishop's face. He stood up and walked to the window. He pulled the tan curtain back and stared outside for a moment. Then he turned back to JT and said, "You have problems at the church also, JT. Having Deacon Benson attack you and tell everyone that his wife left him because she had a baby by you is something I can't ignore."

"I'm not stupid, Bishop! I know I messed up. But I think I can turn things around."

"Don't you get it, JT? There are consequences for your actions."

Since meeting Bishop Turner, JT had always thought of the man as the father he never had. Bishop had groomed him for leadership, and when the time was right, he'd introduced him to his wife and given him a church to preside over. Now he was standing in his room looking like JT was the prodigal who hadn't yet come home. The disappointment on the man's face brought shame to JT. He turned away, not wanting to look Bishop in the face. "So, you didn't come here to see how I'm doing. You're here to give me my consequences, is that it?"

"Don't blame this on me, JT. I'm not your enemy. I've treated you like a son, and look how you've repaid my kindness. Look how you treated Cassandra."

JT looked at the ceiling as he said, "No matter what I've done or what you think of me, I do love my wife. And I'm sorry that I hurt her."

Bishop Turner sat back down. He put his elbow on his

thigh while rubbing his head with his hand. He leaned back in his seat and told JT, "I came here to tell you that Elder Unders will be taking over your responsibilities at the church while you recuperate."

"And when I'm done recuperating?"

"I don't know, JT. I think we're going to need to take this one day at a time."

JT was pensive for a moment as his mind went back to that day in Vivian's bathroom when he looked in her mirror and saw a monster. He turned to Bishop and asked him, "Have you ever felt forsaken by God?"

Bishop blinked. He sat up straight and adjusted his tie. "I don't know how to answer that question, JT."

"God has given up on me. Matter of fact, I even think I heard God tell me that He had forsaken me." JT looked at Bishop and added, "I don't want to be forsaken, but I don't know what to do about it."

"Seek God, JT."

"I've been trying to do that. But He's not listening to me anymore." JT was obviously frustrated as he hit the bed with his free arm.

"JT, you've read your Bible from front to back more times than I can count. So I know that you are aware of the saints who have disappointed God at one time or another. Those saints might have been disciplined by God, but they were also forgiven." Bishop Turner stood up and put his hand on JT's arm. "Don't give up, son. Don't let it end like this."

Cassandra did her best to put the past out of her mind and take care of her husband. JT was in constant pain the first month, so it was easy to have compassion for his situation. Although, she did have her "mad black woman" moments when she thought about letting him starve to death, or not bathing him until he passed out from the strong smell of stank. On those days, she was glad that JT had a physical therapist coming to the house several times a week to check on him. If nothing else, that made her get up and take care of him even when she didn't want to. Right now, Cassandra couldn't say for sure if she took care of JT because she still loved him. As far as she was concerned, JT had destroyed the love she had for him when adultery had become his extracurricular activity.

She was sitting down in the kitchen talking to her mother, trying to make sense of her life. But nothing made sense anymore. Cassandra put her elbow on the table and her hand on her head as she told her mother, "I just don't know what to do."

"It ain't all that confusing to me. Put the bum out," Mattie told her.

"Mom, where is your heart? JT can't even get out of that bed right now. He's in so much pain he can barely see straight."

Mattie stood up and hit Cassandra in the back of her head. "Where's your backbone? Why do you have to be this man's doormat?"

Cassandra put her hand on the back of her head. "Ouch, that hurts."

"Well, then why don't you get up and do something about it?" Mattie said.

Cassandra's mother was no more than five feet tall, but she acted like a giant most of the time. Mattie had put the fear of God in Cassandra early on, so even after she had grown taller than her mother, she wouldn't dream of hitting her. "It's not as if I'm going to hit you back," Cassandra told her.

Mattie flailed her arms in the air, exasperated. "I'm not talking about me. I want you to fight back against this no-good man who's living under your roof."

"What am I supposed to do, Mama? My youngest child

is eleven months, I don't have a job, and JT pays all the bills."

Mattie put her hands on her hips and said, "The man just had a baby on you, Cassandra. Any judge worth his salt would tell JT that he has to keep paying these bills."

Cassandra stood up. She had a bowl of ham and bean soup. "I've got to give JT his lunch and a pain pill."

Mattie shoved Cassandra back in her seat. "You will do no such thing. You are going to sit here and rest while them boys are taking a nap. I'll go check on that adulterer."

"Mom, be nice," Cassandra said, putting her feet up on the chair next to her.

As Mattie took the tray out of the cabinet she asked Cassandra, "Would it be nice if I don't put rat poison in his soup?"

"Of course it would."

"Well then, I'm being nice. Because that's what I'd like to do for him," she said as she put the soup on the tray, took a glass out of the cabinet, and poured him some 7UP. "Where are his pain pills?"

Cassandra picked up the pills from the table and handed them to Mattie. "Remember, Mama, be nice."

Mattie rolled her eyes as she walked out of the kitchen, and headed to the guest bedroom. "How are you feeling?" Mattie asked, forcing a smile as she opened the door.

"Like I got hit by a car," JT said with a half-hearted smile.

"Mmh," Mattie said as she walked into the room and put the tray down on the dresser. "That's about how Cassandra felt when the mother of your illegitimate child came to the hospital demanding to see you."

"That woman's child does not belong to me," JT proclaimed.

"Yeah, that's what your mouth says. But get a DNA test and we'll see whose chickens come home to roost," Mattie said. When JT didn't respond, Mattie flat-out asked, "When can we expect that DNA test?"

"That's between me and my wife. This is none of your business."

Mattie pulled the spoon from the soup and held it like a weapon. She then looked at the so-called weapon in her hand and put it back in the soup. She told JT, "You better be glad I don't have a knife on me, because I would stab you until I got tired. Then I would stand here and watch you bleed to death before I dialed 911."

"Cassandra! Cassandra!" JT screamed.

"Why are you hollering for my daughter? You're no better than a piece of dirt. You don't deserve her."

"She's my wife."

"I tried to warn her about you preacher types. I'm just sorry that she didn't listen to me."

Cassandra opened the door. "What's wrong, JT?"

"Your mother just threatened to stab me to death. Can you please get her out of our house?" JT said.

"Your house?" Mattie laughed. "Boy, after Cassandra gets finished telling the judge everything you've done to her, you won't even be able to afford to live in a shoe."

JT leaned his head back. The pain that shot through his body was written all over his face. He yelled through the pain, "Get her out of here!"

"Come on, Mama. I asked you to be nice," Cassandra said as she escorted her mother out of the guest room.

"What are you talking about? I didn't poison him. I only suggested what I would do if I had a knife." Mattie raised her hands in the air and turned them from front to back. "Do I have a knife?"

"Oh, Mother, you are truly a character. I honestly don't

know how you avoid getting arrested. Wait for me in the kitchen, please," Cassandra said as she left Mattie on the opposite side of the door and closed it.

"Did she give you the soup?" Cassandra asked, turning back to JT.

"No, she was too busy trying to use the spoon as a knife."

Cassandra picked up the bowl and brought it over to JT. "I need you to eat this so you can take your pain pill."

"Thank you for doing this for me. I appreciate what you're doing."

Surprised by JT's thankful attitude, Cassandra stood in front of him for a moment, unsure of what to do or say next.

"I can feed myself if you want. My arm is feeling a lot stronger today," JT told her.

Cassandra looked down at the bowl of soup in her hands. "You only have one hand free. You won't be able to hold the bowl and feed yourself until the cast comes off of your other arm." She sat down next to the bed and began feeding him. But as she sat there, her eyes didn't travel past his mouth. She didn't want to look in his eyes; didn't want to feel anything for this man. Cassandra just wanted to help him get through the healing process so they could get on with the business of getting a divorce.

"Why don't we talk to each other anymore, Sanni?" JT asked between mouthfuls of soup.

She put the soup down and put her hands in her lap. "I don't know what to say to you."

"I'm sorry, Sanni. I know I messed up. I destroyed my credibility at the church, and my relationship with you and God." A sharp pain shot through him and he shifted position in the bed.

Cassandra saw the strained look on his face and real-

ized that she had let too much time lapse since his last
pain pill. She had left his pain pills and 7UP on the dresser.
"Let me get your pain pills," she told JT as she stood,
picked up his pills and 7UP and returned to the side of his
bed. She handed him two pills and the glass. "Take these,
then you should be able to take a nap without so much
pain."

"That's the problem. Every time I take these pills I fall
asleep."

Cassandra took the glass from JT's hand after he swallowed the pain pills. "I'm going to check on the kids. You
get some sleep and I'll bring them in to see you later this
evening," she told him. She walked out of his room as fast
as she could without appearing to run.

When JT opened his eyes again, the evening news was
on the television. The news was depressing as usual. The
newscaster talked with people who were in the process of
losing their homes. They covered stories about theft and
murder, and for the first time in a long time, JT actually
cared. His heart went out to these people who were being
thrown out of their homes, and to the murder victims. His
eyes shifted heavenward as he asked God, "Where is the
church while all of this is going on, Lord?"

JT rolled his eyes as he realized that he already knew
the answer to his question. The church was out buying
bigger homes and fabulous cars, and just being blessed.
The church was too busy worrying about how America's
current economic downturn would affect them to feel
compassion or try to help others less fortunate. JT was
just like them. He'd lost his compassion for a hurting
world. But lying in his bed, watching tragedy unfold via
the evening news, JT wanted to not only feel compassion
for these people, he wanted to do something about it. For

the first time in a long time, his eyes filled with tears for someone other than himself.

JT's bedroom door opened and Jerome ran in. "Daddy, Daddy, look what I have." Jerome lifted his hands to display his new football. "Mommy bought it for me."

JT wiped away the tears from his face. "That's nice, son. I can't wait to throw that ball to you," JT told him as he looked up to see Cassandra walking into his room with his youngest son, Aaron, in her arms.

The three people in JT's life that should have mattered most were in the room with him. But one of them wanted nothing to do with him anymore. He looked at Cassandra and saw the woman he had fallen in love with almost ten years ago.

They met at a church revival in Memphis. JT had been attending and ministering at a small church in Alabama over which Bishop Turner presided. Bishop had asked JT to attend the revival; told him that he wanted to discuss his future in the ministry.

JT arrived at church late, so he sat in the back and listened to the pastor deliver his message of hope to the congregation. When the service was over, JT got up to find Bishop Turner. When he reached the front of the church, he saw Turner, but he also noticed a young woman standing next to him. Her hair was cut in a bob with bronze streaks that complimented her honey-toned complexion.

JT walked up to Bishop Turner and shook his hand. He said, "Hello, sir," while staring at Cassandra.

Bishop laughed as he brought forward the woman next to him. "Hello, JT. Let me introduce you to my goddaughter. This is Cassandra Daniels."

Cassandra shook JT's hand as she said, "Nice to meet you. The bishop has told me all about his new preacher from Alabama. It sounds like you walk on water."

"No," JT said. "I'm just dumb enough to step out on the water and sink with the best of them."

Cassandra laughed.

JT liked the sound of her laugh. But he noticed that even though there was a smile on her face, her brown eyes still looked sad. From that moment, JT made it his business to put a sparkle in her eyes.

Cassandra sat down next to JT's bed with Aaron in her arms. Jerome ran around the room tossing his football in the air.

JT turned to Cassandra and asked, "Remember what I told you the night we got engaged?"

Cassandra looked confused. "What?"

Adjusting himself in the bed so that he faced his wife, JT said, "I was driving you home and you laughed at something I said. There was a sparkle in your eyes that hadn't been there before, remember?"

Cassandra bit her lip as she nodded.

"I told you that for the rest of my life, I would move the world to keep that sparkle in your eyes."

Cassandra's eyes were overshadowed with sadness as she said, "Yeah, I remember that."

Even though JT's right arm was no longer in the sling, it still hurt him to move it. But he stretched out his arm and squeezed her hand as a tear fell from his eyes. "I'm sorry I didn't keep my promise."

CHAPTER 16

JT was now sitting up, able to get out of bed and move around a little bit. Nothing major, but he was definitely on the mend.

Betty came to see him, and JT was able to sit in the living room and talk with her.

"Praise the Lord!" Betty exclaimed. "I prayed that you would recover from that horrible accident."

"Thank you for calling to check on me. Cassandra told me how many times you called. And thanks for the tuna casserole you brought over the other night."

"Not a problem. I just wish I could have done more."

JT waved his hand. "You've done more than enough for my family."

She opened her briefcase and pulled out the files she'd brought with her. "Elder Unders is doing a good job in your absence. He wanted to come out to see you, but I told him that Cassandra has limited your visitors so you can recuperate."

"It was probably for the best. I would have been running my big mouth and not resting, causing Cassandra to have to do everything around the house for a much longer time."

Betty laughed. "Yeah, you need to get back on your feet so you can do dishes and Cassandra can take a break.

"I'm allergic to dish water. I'm more a vacuum-the-floor and make-the-beds kind of guy," JT said, then he pointed at the files in Betty's hand. "What did you bring me?"

"I thought you'd like to see the offering totals for this month. I also brought you the ministry activity list."

JT took the files from Betty and looked through them. He had become pastor of Faith Outreach almost eight years ago. At the time, the church only had three hundred members. But the last five years had seen explosive growth. They now had thirty-five hundred members, which equated to about $15 million in giving per year. "The giving is down this month," JT said, studying the report.

"Yes, Pastor. We normally bring in about $1.5 million, except for slow months like June and January. But we only brought in nine hundred thousand this month."

"Do you know why that might be?"

Betty looked away from JT and lowered her eyes as she responded, "We've lost a lot of members since you've been away."

JT looked shocked. "No one told me that. Why are they leaving?"

Betty still didn't look at JT. "Vivian has been telling people that you and she had a relationship, and that you started stalking her when she broke it off."

"That's not true," JT said, knowing full well that part of her story was indeed true.

"Elder Unders wants to fire her, but he needs your approval."

JT was angry. Vivian was trying to destroy him. "Tell him to fire her immediately."

"There's one other thing, Pastor." Betty pulled a fax

from her briefcase and handed it to him. "Senator Grassley has contacted us again. He wants to review our books."

JT put his hand on his forehead and rubbed his temple. "I may have done a lot of things, Betty. But I never stole from the church."

"Why don't we just give them the information they want? Then maybe they'll leave us alone."

JT had a headache. He really needed this nightmare to be over. "Let me think about it, Betty. I'll let you know."

Betty closed her briefcase and stood up. "I don't want to overtax you today, so I'll just come back in a few days."

JT was still rubbing his temple with his eyes closed. "All right. Let's talk in a couple of days."

"You look so sad, Pastor. Is there anything I can do for you?"

He wished with all that was in him that someone could do something to help him. JT couldn't point to a time in his life when he had felt this alone. When his mother died on him, he thought he had Mona. When he discovered that Mona was cheating on him, JT had hung with Jimmy. When Jimmy got himself arrested and JT feared that he would be arrested also, he had turned to God. But now God had turned away from him. JT knew he was sunk and there was nothing he could do about it. Then an idea struck him and he lifted his head with excitement. He asked Betty, "Do you know how to get a prayer through to God?"

"Excuse me, Pastor?"

"You know what I mean. God doesn't hear everybody's prayers." JT knew that first hand, since God had stopped listening to him. "You've got to have a clean heart and clean hands."

She was silent.

"Is your heart clean before God, Betty?"

"I believe it is, Pastor."

Humbly he asked, "Then would you pray for me?"

Stumbling over her words, she told him, "Y—yes, Pastor. I will fast and pray."

Betty walked out of the living room and went into the kitchen to say goodbye to Cassandra. JT looked to heaven. "You might ignore me, but you can't ignore everybody. You have to honor Your word. The prayers of the righteous avail much. Remember those words, Lord?"

God had given up on him. He'd slid the final nail in his coffin the day he slept with Vivian. He understood that. But just because God had turned His back on him, did that mean he had to give up the fight? Did he have to stop loving God? Because the truth of the matter was, JT did love God. He meant every word he'd said the day he gave his life to the Lord. Somehow things just got messed up and he'd forgotten all that he'd promised the Lord.

An idea struck him and he lifted his head with excitement. Jim Baker and other preachers like him had been forsaken by God; the whole world could attest to that. But JT had seen Jim Baker after he'd been released from prison. "Anointed" was the word that crossed his mind when he looked at the resurrected Jim Baker. And God was no respecter of persons, right?

JT turned his head toward heaven and with tears running down his face, he cried out, "God, you've been so good to me through the years. You've seen me through some tough times. So, even though I know I've done wrong, I just can't walk away. I'll spend the rest of my life proving to You that I want to change. Not only do I want to change, Lord, but from this moment on, I declare to You that I am a changed man. And now all I want to do is search out Your will for my life."

JT went to his room and picked up his Bible. He had an overwhelming need to read God's Word; a need to be cleansed. So it was no surprise that he turned to Psalm 51.

> *Have mercy upon me, O God, according to thy loving kindness: according unto the multitude of thy tender mercies, blot out my transgressions.*
> *Wash me thoroughly from mine iniquity, and cleanse me from my sin.*
> *For I acknowledge my transgressions: and my sin is ever before me.*
> *Against thee, thee only, have I sinned, and done this evil . . .*

JT laid his Bible on his lap and looked heavenward as he examined this truth. JT knew he had sinned and done so repeatedly. But in all that he had done, JT had never once considered that simple truth: that his sins put him at odds with God. Standing behind his pulpit, preaching God's Word, meant nothing, because he was living contrary to the Word he preached. He turned back to his Bible and continued to read:

> *Purge me with hyssop and I shall be clean: wash me and I shall be whiter than snow.*
> *Make me to hear joy and gladness: that the bones which thou hast broken may rejoice.*
> *Hide thy face from my sins, and blot out all mine iniquities.*
> *Create in me a clean heart, O God; and renew a right spirit within me.*
> *Cast me not away from thy presence: and take not thy holy spirit from me.*

JT leaned his head against the back of the chair and closed his eyes. He never imagined that separating from God would be so painful. But it was. JT thought that losing his baby girl was the most pain he would ever feel in this life. But now that years had gone by, he'd learned to live with her absence. But could he learn to live with the absence of God, and did he want to? "Oh God," he said. "I know that You have already taken your presence from me. But I can't live without You."

He got out of his chair and stretched out on his bed. JT wanted to stretch out on the floor, but he wasn't sure if he would be able to get up without help. Tears were flowing from his eyes. JT realized that he had been crying a lot lately. "Lord, please create in me a clean heart." He was sobbing now as he said, "I—I don't w—want to live without You."

Cassandra opened his bedroom door and rushed into the room. "Are you okay?"

"No," JT answered honestly as he wiped the tears from his eyes. "But I won't stop pleading my case before the Lord until I am okay again."

CHAPTER 17

The next morning, JT got out of bed, walked down the hall, and stood at the bottom of the stairs. He wanted to walk up those stairs but he wasn't totally steady on his feet yet, so he yelled, "Cassandra!"

When there was no answer, he yelled again, "Cassandra!"

Cassandra unlocked her bedroom door and walked into the hall. She stood at the top of the stairs with her finger over her mouth. "Shh. The boys are still sleeping."

"Can you look for some of the ministry tapes I used to listen to and my tape player? They're in our walk-in closet in our bedroom."

She looked toward her bedroom and then turned back to JT. "Can I get them for you when the boys wake up?"

"Are they sleeping in our bedroom? I thought we agreed not to get that started with them?"

She didn't look at JT as she responded, "I don't like sleeping by myself."

JT thought her comment was an invitation for him. He leaned against the stair post and said, "Maybe you should move to the bedroom downstairs with me. Until I'm able to climb these stairs, I won't be able to sleep in our bedroom with you."

She rolled her eyes at that suggestion, turned, walked back into her room, and closed the door. JT heard her turn the lock before he turned and walked away. He went to his home office, which, thankfully, was on the first floor. He sat down in his wingback swivel chair and began searching through his desk drawers for CDs and cassettes of some of his favorite preachers. He wished he had full use of both arms and couldn't wait until the cast was taken off his right arm. But since he was pretty much on his own, as evidenced by Cassandra locking her bedroom door, he had to make do with the one arm he had.

The first thing his hand passed over while searching through his top drawer was a picture of Sarah. He picked it up and leaned back in his seat. He had taken this picture with the camera he'd brought into the delivery room. They had pronounced his baby dead, but he still needed something to remember her by, so he'd snapped the picture.

He kept Sarah's picture in his desk drawer as a constant reminder of the day God failed him. Each time he opened that drawer and looked at her unmoving form, JT felt vindicated in his wrongdoings. After all, he had something on God, so how could the Almighty call him on anything that he had done?

However, today JT didn't feel like kicking against the prick anymore. Looking at his first child's picture, he said, "I'll never forget you, Sarah. I'm so sorry that you aren't here with us, but I have to move on. I can't hold your death against God anymore." He then placed the picture underneath some files in the bottom drawer.

The Purpose and Power of God's Glory tape by Myles Munroe was already in his tape recorder, as if God knew what he needed to listen to first. He leaned back in his seat and listened to Myles Munroe explain how humans exist to manifest God's glory. JT was intrigued by the concept. Then Myles Munroe started talking about the glory of becoming what God has called us to be, and JT was swept away. He'd often wondered if pastoring a church was truly the thing God wanted from him. He loved to preach, but didn't feel as if he was all that good with the administrative part of his job. JT decided that he would put that question on his prayer list. He didn't even worry about the fact that God wasn't answering his prayers right now. He had decided last night that he was going to bombard heaven with so many prayers, God would have to answer.

When the Myles Monroe tape finished, JT listened to Joyce Myers discuss discipline in the life of a Christian. After that tape, JT needed to take a break. He went into the kitchen to get a bowl of bran cereal and a banana, before going back into his office to continue feasting on the Word of God.

Cassandra was in front of the stove cooking oatmeal and Jerome was at the kitchen table when JT walked in. Jerome got up from the table and ran to JT. "Daddy, Daddy," he yelled as he wrapped his arms around JT.

"Good morning, son. Did you sleep well?"

"Yes!" he said as if he were cheering for his favorite football team. Jerome then asked. "Daddy, why don't you sleep in Mommy's room anymore?"

"Sit back down, Jerome. Your oatmeal is ready," Cassandra said just before turning to JT. "I'll get your tapes out of the room in a little while; Aaron is still asleep."

JT smiled as he noted how easy Cassandra was able to get Jerome's mind off of them and on his tummy. Jerome sat down, grabbed his spoon, and waited for his bowl. "I can wait. I found some tapes in my office," JT said as he went to the cabinet and grabbed a bowl. "I just came in here to get a bowl of cereal and some fruit before I go back." He looked at Jerome. "Can I sit with you, champ?"

Jerome smiled. "Yes, Daddy, come sit with me."

As JT sat down at the table, Cassandra said, "I'm going to go check on Aaron."

"Okay, Sanni. Jerome and I will entertain ourselves while you're gone."

Cassandra stopped in her tracks. She used to love when JT called her Sanni, but she was sick and tired of him taking privileges that he no longer deserved. She turned back to JT and said, "Please don't call me Sanni. Just call me Cassandra. Okay?"

Cassandra was fuming. JT had no right to use the nickname he'd given her years ago. "How dare he," she said as she flopped down on her bed. She was stuck in this house with him for the time being, but she would no longer put up with him acting as if she were someone special to him. This man had single-handedly ruined her life. She had put up with so much mess from him. After their baby girl died, JT did not comfort her. No, he spent his time cheating on her with one woman after another. And now that he was hurt, she was supposed to just forgive and forget all of JT's transgressions. She picked up a pillow from her bed, put it against her face, and screamed. Aaron jerked and started screaming also. Cassandra stood, walked over to his crib, and picked him up. She looked to heaven as she rocked Aaron in her arms and said, "I'm sorry for scaring you, little one."

She grabbed a diaper and the wet wipes, laid Aaron on her bed, and changed his diaper. All the while she noticed that Aaron looked more like his father with each passing day. But she wasn't holding that against her baby. She loved her children and wouldn't care who they looked like. But she was really tired of seeing JT. The way she was feeling right now, she could go a lifetime without seeing him again. Cassandra wouldn't throw him out in his time of need, but she really didn't know how she would get through the next few weeks.

She took Aaron downstairs. After JT spent a little time playing with him, Cassandra fed her youngest. Jerome went with JT back to his office. Cassandra was glad when JT walked out of the kitchen. Her irritation with him had begun first thing this morning when he asked her to move into his bedroom with him. What in the world would make JT think she wanted to sleep with him?

She walked over to the sink and ran some water. She was still fuming as she put the breakfast dishes in the water, so she started talking to God again. "I love You, Lord. But I swear I don't understand You at all. JT does all this awful stuff to me, even getting some woman pregnant. And now he's praying and crying to You, listening to tapes about You, and trying to act as if he's sorry for the things he's done. I just don't believe it, Lord."

"I don't blame you for being angry with me," JT said as he stood in the kitchen.

Cassandra turned toward the door, embarrassed that she had been caught talking to God about JT. So, she testily said, "Are you sneaking up on people now?"

"I'm sorry, I didn't mean to scare you."

She waved him off. "No use apologizing for scaring me. Believe me, you've done much worse than that."

Leaning against the wall, JT told her, "I am trying to change, Cassandra. I can't make any promises, though. You deserve better than empty promises from me."

Cassandra took Aaron out of his highchair. "I'm going to get the kids dressed and go to the grocery store."

"Do you mind if I come with you? I'd like to stop at Best Buy or a Christian bookstore so I can pick up a few gospel CDs."

Cassandra rolled her eyes, but said, "That's fine. I'll take you wherever you need to go." She was going to show him who was the real Christian between the two of them. *I can be charitable*, she thought as she brushed passed him without looking his way.

CHAPTER 18

They went to the Christian bookstore first. Cassandra was carrying Aaron, while holding Jerome's hand. JT had to walk with his cane, and since he still had the cast, he wasn't much help with the kids. The Thomases were well-known in this store because they bought most of their Christian material here. JT also encouraged his members to shop at Christian Light.

The manager of the store ran over to JT and Cassandra. She hugged Cassandra and then said to JT, "Pastor Thomas, we were so worried about you. Thank God you survived that accident."

"Thank you, Becky. I'm mending," JT told her.

"How long does your arm have to be in that cast?" Becky asked

JT put his hand on his cast as he responded, "Probably just another month."

Cassandra reminded him, "That's not what the doctor said." Cassandra turned to Becky. "The doctor will check his arm in about a month to see if it's healed enough to come out of the cast."

Becky smiled at Cassandra and JT and then asked, "So, what brings you two in the store today?"

"I need some more gospel CDs," JT told her.

"Well, don't let me stop you." Becky pointed toward the CDs. "You know where everything is. If we don't have something you're looking for, just let me know and I'll order them for you."

"Thanks," JT said as he walked over to the CDs. He and Cassandra looked through them, ruled out a few, but managed to find some they both wanted to listen to. When they were through, they had CDs by Donnie McClurkin, Cee Cee Winans, Fred Hammond, Martha Munizzi, and Smokie Norful.

As they walked out of the Christian bookstore, JT told Cassandra, "I'd like for us to play this music throughout the house during the day. Would that be okay with you?"

Cassandra's eyebrow went up. "Since when do you care what I want to do in our house?"

JT touched Cassandra's arm, stopping her from walking into the street toward their car. He waited until she looked at him before speaking. "I do care what you think, Cassandra. It may have seemed like I didn't care, but that person wasn't the real me."

Cassandra didn't respond. She walked toward the car and unlocked the door.

JT opened the back door so Jerome could climb in. He got into the passenger side while Cassandra strapped the kids into their car seats. When he looked out of his window, he saw Vivian Sampson in the car in front of them. She was staring at him with hate-filled eyes. A cold chill went down JT's spine as he watched Vivian back out of her parking spot and speed off.

"Good Lord, why would someone peel out of a parking lot like that? Don't they know that children walk around here?" Cassandra said as she got in the car and put her seat belt on.

"Usually it's some nut that acts like that," JT said, convinced now more than ever that Vivian was not only nuts, but a stalker as well.

Cassandra turned to JT and asked, "So are you up to going with me to the grocery store?"

"Can we go to the grocery store tomorrow? I'd like to talk to you about some things if that's okay."

They arrived home at noon, fed the children lunch, and Cassandra took Jerome and Aaron upstairs so they could take a nap. Once they were asleep, she came back downstairs.

JT was in the family room listening to Cece Winans sing "Alabaster Box." He leaned his head back against the couch and soaked in the story of a woman who was a sinner, but came to Jesus in a repentant manner and had been forgiven.

"Okay, I'm here. What did you want to talk about?" Cassandra asked when she walked into the family room.

He patted the seat next to him. "Sit down with me, Cassandra."

She sat down, but not on the couch next to JT. Cassandra sat in the chair next to the couch. "I'm listening."

He'd brought this on himself, so he couldn't blame Cassandra for how distant she had become. He had grown distant himself when Sarah died, and now he needed to explain. He took a deep breath and said, "I know you feel as if I kind of checked out of our family. But to tell you the truth, when Sarah died, I got lost. I just didn't know how to handle it."

"Oh, so I guess I wasn't hurt by the death of my baby?" Cassandra said, rolling her eyes in exasperation.

JT raised his hand to try to stop Cassandra from getting

angry. "I know you were hurt. What I'm trying to tell you is that I lost my way with God after Sarah died. I probably should have stepped down from my role as pastor, but I was too prideful to admit that I didn't trust God. So, I acted out in other ways."

"Are you referring to how you got someone else pregnant?"

JT lowered his head as he admitted, "That and other things. But I've got to tell you, Cassandra, I don't think Diane's baby is mine. I contacted my attorney and asked him to set up a DNA test. So if you can just hang on long enough for me to take a DNA test, I'll prove to you that I'm not the father of her baby."

A tear rolled down Cassandra's cheek. She wiped it away. "Are you kidding, JT? Do you really think I care if some test proves that you're not the father of that baby? My problem is the fact that you even have to take the test."

"I'm sorry about that, Cassandra."

"Yeah, you're real sorry. And I suppose I should fall all over myself forgiving you?"

He leaned closer to her and put his hand on her thigh. She brushed it off. "I can't turn back the clock, Cassandra. But if you give me a chance, I will try my best to make all of this up to you."

"How in the world do you think you can make any of this up to me? My mother thinks I'm a fool for allowing you to recuperate in our home."

Angrily, JT said, "Your mother thought you were a fool for marrying me in the first place."

"And didn't you prove her right?" Cassandra shook her head and stood up. "Look, maybe it's too soon for us to try to have a civilized conversation."

JT raised his hands again. "Please don't leave. I'm trying to finally inject some truth into our relationship.

Maybe we won't ever be able to get back together, but I need you to know that the things I did were never about you, it was all about me."

Cassandra sat back down. "I'm listening."

"First off, I think the reason things began to unravel for us after Sarah died is because I didn't start our marriage off right in the first place. I wasn't truthful with you."

"Are you referring to the reason you postponed our wedding two times? Are you finally going to fess up to what that was all about? Because I'd really like to know."

"Yes, Cassandra, I'm going to tell you everything. But you have to promise to sit here and listen to me. What I'm going to say isn't going to be easy for you, but you have to promise to stay and listen. Deal?"

She twisted her lip in contemplation, then said, "Fine."

JT took a deep breath. He lowered his head, closed his eyes, and put his steepled hands under his chin.

"Out with it, JT. You weren't praying while you were doing all your dirt, so please spare me the theatrics."

JT opened his eyes and said, "Remember you promised that you would stay and listen." When Cassandra didn't respond, JT trod on. "Okay, see, I knew you always thought that I was having second thoughts about marrying you when I postponed our wedding, but it was never like that." He gulped and blurted out, "I was married when we met."

"What?" Cassandra exploded as she jumped out of her seat.

"You said you would listen, remember?"

Cassandra plopped back down. She waved her hand impatiently in the air. "Please continue. I can't wait to hear the rest of this."

JT felt like a caged animal. He thought telling the truth would make things better between him and Cassandra, but maybe some truths were better left unsaid. But JT had determined that he wanted a clean heart, so this was some of that hyssop the Lord was using to purge him. If he had been honest with Cassandra before they got married, who knew what would have happened between them when Sarah died? Maybe JT would have even confided in his wife his feelings of doubt, rather than seeking out the comfort of other women. "I told you about the night my mother died and how Jimmy and I robbed this drug dealer. But I didn't tell you the reason we robbed him." He looked over at Cassandra to see if she was listening. She was turned to the side, facing the wall, not looking his way. "When I went home to tell Mona—"

"Who is Mona?" Cassandra asked, still facing the wall.

"My first wife's name is Mona. Anyway, when I went home to tell her what happened to my mother, she was in bed with Lester Grayson, the drug dealer Jimmy and I robbed."

"I knew it. When you told me that story about robbing that drug dealer I knew that you weren't telling me the whole story. You might be a lot of things, but you're no thief."

"Well, I became one that night," he told her. Then Cassandra turned to face him. JT saw the mistrust in her eyes, kind of like how he had stopped trusting God. He understood her, and even felt her pain. He had already decided that he would fight his way back to God, and now he was just as determined to fight his way back into Cassandra's heart.

"You robbed that man for her. This woman you used to be married to." The way Cassandra said those words sounded like she was complaining that JT took someone else to the prom, while she sat at home waiting on him.

Waving his hands in the air as if calling a timeout, JT said, "Wait a minute, Cassandra. This isn't about Mona. I'm trying to tell you what happened before we got married."

Cassandra didn't say anything. She just rolled her eyes and leaned back in her seat.

"This guy we robbed was real angry and word got around that he wanted to kill me. So I never went back to New Orleans, nor did I contact Mona about a divorce; until I met you. I had my attorney send her divorce papers, but she contacted him and said that she wouldn't give me a divorce until I sat down with her face-to-face. She asked for my address, and thankfully my attorney refused to give it to her."

"Why wouldn't she just sign the papers? Did she want to get back with you or something?"

"Hardly," JT said with a bitter laugh. "She was still with Lester and she wanted me back in New Orleans so he could kill me."

Cassandra took a sharp breath, but quickly recovered so that she could continue looking at him with loathing.

"I was sorry about postponing our wedding, but I was trying to find a way to get this divorce done without getting myself killed. But then about a month before our third wedding date, Lester was murdered and Mona needed money. She asked me for my entire score from that robbery, the whole hundred and twenty-five thousand, and I gave it to her without blinking an eye."

With an eyebrow raised, Cassandra said, "How could you have held onto that money for all those years?"

"You don't get it, do you? After I gave my life to God I didn't want the money. I really can't tell you why I held on to it. Maybe I was worried that I wouldn't be able to make an honest living. I put the money in a safe deposit box and left it alone. But I wanted you so bad, that when Mona asked for my cut, I gave it to her without a second thought."

"Do you think that moves me, JT? I wish you had never given her the money. I wish you had stayed married to her.

It sounds like the two of you deserve each other," Cassandra said as she stood up and walked out of the room.

JT wanted to call her back. He had so much more he wanted to tell her, but he recognized that he'd already unloaded a ton of manure on her, and Cassandra needed to get away from the stench.

CHAPTER 19

On Tuesday morning, JT received two calls that were supposed to be good news, but the calls only made him think more about his misguided past. The first call came from Elder Unders. JT had a great deal of respect for this man. He had been married for twenty-seven years, and had not compromised his marriage with adultery like he had. Elder Unders was a man that God would be proud to call his servant.

"Pastor, I hope this isn't a bad time, but I wanted to let you know that I had to let Vivian Sampson go today."

JT had told Betty to have Unders fire Vivian last week, so he asked, "What took you so long?"

"Well," Unders began with a bit of hesitation. "From what I was told, Vivian had reason to say some of the things she's been saying. So, I tried to work with her, first by telling her that her behavior was unacceptable, and that if it continued she would have to find other employment."

Had things really gotten this bad? Was JT now expected to put up with an elder at his church talking down to him?

JT shook off the anger at the situation as he realized that he had brought all of this on himself. He then asked Elder Unders, "What was the final straw with her?"

"Look, Pastor, I'd rather not go into all of this with you. I called Bishop Turner and told him what's been going on around here, so you might be receiving a call from him soon."

"He already called. I'm having lunch with him later this week," JT said.

"Well, all right then, Pastor. I hope you come back to church real soon."

"As a matter of fact, I was going to see if Cassandra would bring me to church this Sunday. You've always preached some good messages, and I need to be ministered to right now."

There was silence on the line for a moment, then Elder Unders said, "I think the Lord would be pleased with that, Pastor."

"See you soon, Unders," JT said.

Unders hung up without saying good-bye. JT respected Unders, but he realized from the way their conversation had gone that Unders had lost respect for him. JT was busy working on regaining respect from God and Cassandra, so he didn't have time to add anyone else to the list right now.

JT stood up and grabbed his cane, getting ready to walk out of his office, when the phone rang again. He sat back down and picked up the phone. "This is JT."

"Hello, Mr. Thomas, this is Officer McDaniels. How are you doing?"

"I've been worse," JT said.

"Well, I'm calling to give you some good news. I think we caught the guy who ran you over."

"You've got Jimmy?"

"Yes, sir. But he already had a warrant out for his arrest

when we picked him up, so we need you to come down here and identify him before we have to release him to New Orleans."

"When do you need me?"

"Today, if you can get down here. How about three o'clock?" Officer McDaniels asked.

"I'll see if my wife can drive me," JT told him just before they hung up. He went to find Cassandra. She was upstairs. JT had been trying not to climb up and down the stairs, since his leg was still giving him problems. At the bottom of the stairs, JT yelled, "Cassandra, can you come down here for a minute?"

She yelled back, "Give me a minute. I'm changing Aaron."

"Okay, I'll wait for you in the living room," JT told her as he headed to the living room to sit down and wait.

"What's up?" Cassandra asked as she entered the living room carrying Aaron, while Jerome walked behind her flying his toy airplane.

"The police just called. They have Jimmy, but they need me to come and identify him as the person who ran me over."

"Thank God," Cassandra said.

JT laughed as he said, "I'm surprised that you're happy about that. I thought you might want Jimmy to run me over again."

Cassandra's hand went to her heart. "How could you say something like that?"

JT waved away his comment. "I'm sorry about that, Cassandra. I'm battling myself on this one. I'm the one who's not as happy as I should be."

Cassandra handed Jerome Aaron's bottle and asked him to put it on the kitchen table. When Jerome shot out of the living room, Cassandra sat down next to JT. "What's going on? Why are you upset about this guy getting arrested?"

JT ran his hands through his wavy, low-cut hair. "I kind of feel like it's my fault that he ran me over."

"That's nonsense, JT."

"No, no, now listen to me. The past few weeks I've been challenging my integrity and I've been holding myself accountable. And when I last met with Jimmy I lied to him." JT looked at Cassandra to gauge her reaction to his admitting that he had lied. There was no surprise on her face, but it wasn't news to him that she knew him to be a liar. He continued, "I told him that I gave his money to Mona so that she would give me a divorce. But that wasn't true. I gave Mona my money; I had held onto Jimmy's money for years. I really didn't want it, and just wanted him to get out of prison and come for it."

"Mommy, can I have an apple?" Jerome asked as he ran back in the room, still flying his airplane.

"Sure, honey, just give me a minute." She turned back to JT and asked, "I'll bite. Why didn't you give him his money if you had been holding onto it all this time?"

"Remember when I bought the Bentley?"

"Yeah, it was right after Sarah died. I remember how you constantly tinkered with that car while I was pretty much left on my own to deal with what happened."

"That's why I bought the car. That's also why I moved us into this house. It helped me not have to deal with what happened to Sarah. I was able to tell our congregation just how much God was blessing us by all the material things we had."

A look of astonishment came over Cassandra's face. "I can't believe you are finally admitting that you bought all this stuff to prove that God still loved us. I always knew it, but you would never admit it."

JT nodded. "I'm admitting it now. But the problem is, I am now being investigated by a congressional board for using church money to fund our fabulous life style."

Rolling her eyes as if to say, "this never ends," Cassandra asked, "When did this happen?"

"The day Jimmy ran me over, the church received a fax about the investigation. But here's the thing, Cassandra. I didn't take any money from the church to buy that car or this house. I used the money I was saving for Jimmy."

"So you robbed your co-conspirator? Wow," Cassandra said. She stood up and walked into the kitchen with Jerome, all the while shaking her head.

JT and Cassandra dropped the kids off at her mother's house and made it to the police station by three o'clock that afternoon. McDaniels took JT in a room behind a one-way mirror. As JT looked through the glass, six men walked into the next room. They each held up a number. There were mostly unfamiliar faces in this lineup. However, JT did recognize the person holding the number four in front of him. It was Jimmy, and he looked as if he'd been sleeping in his car with no mirror for the past three weeks since he had run over JT. His hair was matted to his head on one side and sticking up like Don King's on the other. Jimmy's clothes were tattered and torn. JT lifted his arm and pointed. "That's him. Number four is the one who ran me over."

McDaniels smiled as he pushed the intercom and told the officer on the other side of the glass window, "We're done. You can take them back now."

"What happens now?" JT asked.

McDaniels turned to JT and said, "He's wanted back in New Orleans for armed robbery, so we're still trying to see which location will get to put him on trial first."

"Oh," JT said as they left the room and went back to where Cassandra was waiting for him.

"Are you done?" she asked.

"Yeah, they've got him," JT replied.

"Good," she said as she stood up. "Let's go home."

They went to Mattie's house to pick up the kids. JT stayed in the car, not wanting to have a run in with his mother-in-law. The way he was feeling right now, he would probably hit her with the cast on his right arm and then beat her to death with his cane. With as much as he had to ask forgiveness for, he really didn't need to add another thing to his prayer list.

Cassandra came out with the kids, buckled them in, and they headed home. JT asked, "Did you tell your mom that I said hello?"

"Yes," Cassandra answered without elaborating.

They were silent as they drove home. JT knew that his mother-in-law had probably talked against him while Cassandra was in her house, and Cassandra was probably processing everything that mean, old woman had to say. He wanted Cassandra to forgive him, but he didn't know how to convince her that he was not the same guy he had been just three weeks ago. Truthfully, JT didn't know if the man he had once been would show back up or not. So, the way he saw it, it was best not to boast too much.

When they arrived home and got out of the car, JT noticed a handsomely wrapped package on their doorstep.

"Look, Daddy," Jerome said as he ran toward the front door. "Somebody sent us a present."

The box was wrapped with white paper and tied with a shimmering gold bow. Jerome picked up the box as Cassandra unlocked the door. Wondering who would have left a gift on their doorstep, JT looked around. He spotted a car parked in front of his house on the opposite side of the street. He walked down the lawn as Cassandra and the kids went inside the house. The car looked familiar to him. JT hoped he was wrong, but as he got closer to the car his worst fears were realized. Vivian was sitting behind the wheel.

"What are you doing at my house?" JT asked her.

She laughed at him as she started the car and sped off.

JT turned and headed back to the house. The cane and the pain in his leg made it hard to run, but he hollered, "Don't open that package!"

When he made it to the door, Jerome had already set the package on the table and untied the bow. The paper had been ripped off and Jerome was trying to open it. "No!" JT said as he leaped over to the table and grabbed the box away from Jerome. Agony was etched across JT's face as he fell on the floor. He yelled out in pain.

Cassandra put Aaron in his playpen and turned to JT. "Why would you leap across this room like Superman when you can barely walk as it is?"

He took two deep breaths, trying to ease the pain as he told her, "I just saw Vivian outside our house. I think she left this gift," he said, still holding the package in his hand as if it were a football he'd just stolen from the opposing team.

Cassandra walked over to JT and helped him up onto the couch.

"Can you get me a pain pill?" JT asked Cassandra as he squirmed around on the couch, his face still displaying the pain.

"Yes, I'll be right back," Cassandra told him as she left the room.

"Why can't I open the present, Daddy?" Jerome wanted to know.

"I think this present was meant for Daddy, son. But Mommy and I will get you a present this weekend. Okay?"

"Okay," Jerome said as he ran toward his playroom, quickly forgetting what his heart most desired a second ago.

Cassandra gave JT the pill and a glass of water. He swallowed the pill, then put the package on the table. "I need to open this. I'm not sure if you should be in the room when I do."

"I want to see what she sent you," Cassandra said.

JT opened the box. He first saw an envelope. He removed it from the box and set it on the table. Before reading the note in the envelope, JT had to find out what that God-awful smell he'd just caught a whiff of was. He pulled back the paper that covered the so-called gift, and Cassandra started screaming just as they caught a glimpse of the dead rat that lay in the box, his head hanging loosely from his neck.

Hyperventilating, Cassandra pointed at the box as she moved away from it. "Why would she do this? Why would Vivian give us a rat?"

"There's something wrong with that woman, Cassandra." JT put his hands on his head as he lowered it. "I'm so sorry that I did this to our family," he said, almost in a whisper.

"What does that envelope say?" Cassandra asked as anger permeated her very being.

JT picked it up, opened it, and read, *A dead rat for a filthy rat.*

"Mmph, I guess she's got you pegged," Cassandra said, and walked out of the living room.

CHAPTER 20

JT called the police to report that Vivian was stalking him. The police officer told him that he would have to come down to the station and file the report so he could get a restraining order against Vivian. But JT was in too much pain and feeling a bit worn out from the events of the day to leave the house again. JT went to his bedroom and fell asleep no sooner than his head hit the pillow.

The next morning, JT couldn't get out of bed. Cassandra brought him breakfast and some more pain pills. She asked him, "Do you think you need to go back to the hospital?"

JT shook his head. "I'll be fine. I just think I need to rest today."

"I wish you hadn't leaped across the room like that. You know that you are not fully healed yet." She sat down next to his bed while he ate the eggs, bacon, and biscuits that she had brought him. "I do, however, understand why you did it, and I wanted to thank you for sparing Jerome the trauma of opening something like that."

JT put down his fork and shook his head in sadness. "I

was so scared, Cassandra. I didn't know what else to do. I had no idea what that crazy woman might have put in that box."

Cassandra stood back up, looked away from JT, and said, "Well, if you need anything just use your cell phone to call the house phone in case I'm upstairs and can't hear you call out."

"I think I'm just going to stay in bed and read my Bible. But you can bring some of my ministry tapes and gospel CDs to this room when you get a chance."

She stood by his bedside for a moment with a bewildered expression on her face.

"What's wrong?" he asked.

"Oh, nothing. I was just remembering how you used to study the Bible and listen to your ministry tapes all the time when we were first married."

"I never should have stopped." JT then asked her, "Would you mind driving me to church on Sunday?"

She turned to face him and asked, "Do you think you're up to handling church business right now?"

"I don't want to go to church to preach. I need to be ministered to. I want to sit in the service and listen to Elder Unders."

"You think you can do that?"

JT nodded. "I need to do it. I'm fighting my way back, Cassandra. If you believe nothing else about me, I hope you believe that."

As she turned to walk out of the room, she said to him, "I think I'm starting to believe it."

Cassandra didn't believe in divorce. As a matter of fact, she never even thought the phrase "I want a divorce" would ever cross her lips. But she'd also thought that she would always be a Republican. As a Christian she agreed with the Republican stance on abortion and homosexuality. However, when Barack Obama, a black man, became the Democratic nominee for president of the United States, the Republicans' intolerance and racial attitudes shocked and sickened her. Now, Cassandra considered herself an Independent and felt very comfortable with that label.

So maybe being an independent woman wouldn't be so bad either. As Cassandra stood at the sink washing dishes, she looked around at her beautiful kitchen. She had lovingly picked out the ceramic tile on the floor, the cherry wood cabinets, and the granite counter tops. JT had been right when he bought this house in order to take their minds off of the tragedy they had experienced. Making this house her own had actually helped Cassandra to move past the pain that had settled in her heart after losing her daughter.

She went upstairs and looked in on her children. Opening the door, she remembered the day she and JT found out that she was pregnant with Jerome.

When she left the doctor's office, Cassandra picked up fresh flowers at the florist. She went home, took the vase out of the kitchen cabinet, filled it with water, and put her multi-colored flowers in it setting it on the dining room table. She then set two candles on the table and went back into the kitchen to make dinner. Tonight they were having pork roast, garlic mashed potatoes, and green beans. For dessert, Cassandra fixed peach cobbler.

When JT arrived home from the church, saw the dining room table, and found out what they were having for dinner, he said, "You're not getting ready to tell me that your mother needs to move in with us, are you?"

Cassandra laughed, then said, "I hadn't thought of that, but I can call and ask her if she would like to live with us."

"*No, no. No need to call Mattie, I'd rather just know why you're doing all of this on a Tuesday evening.*"

"*Sit down at the table, sir. I will let you know what's going on in due time,*" *she said as she took their plates to the table.*

JT sat down as Cassandra lit the candles, turned down the lights in the dining room, and then sat down also. "*Do we have any gravy?*" *JT asked.*

"*Oh, I left the gravy bowl on the stove,*" *she said as she started to stand.*

"*Stay seated, I'll get it,*" *JT said. He brought the gravy bowl back to the table and asked,* "*Does my queen need any gravy?*"

She smiled. "*Yes, please put some on my roast and my potatoes.*"

JT did as she requested, then put some gravy on his own plate. He sat down and tasted his food. "*This is really good, honey. Sunday should come on Tuesday more often.*"

"*I don't think I'll be able to work that out for you. I don't know how many other Tuesdays I will find out that I'm pregnant.*"

JT had his face in his plate wolfing down his food. When they were first married, Cassandra used to hate how fast he ate his food. But then he explained to her about going hungry when he was a child. After that discussion, Cassandra never again said anything about the way JT wolfed down his food. Instead, she prayed that God would one day erase JT's past hurts from his mind.

JT dropped his fork. He pushed his chair away from the table and stood up. Walking toward Cassandra he said, "*Did I hear you correctly?*"

She nodded.

JT got down on one knee in front of her chair. Cassan-

dra pushed her chair away from the table and turned toward him. "Are you sure?" JT asked as a tear rolled down his face.

"Yes, honey. It's for real. My doctor confirmed it."

JT laid his head on Cassandra's stomach. He whispered, "Hey you, in there. This is your daddy. I want you to know that even though I just found out about you, I love you already."

Cassandra had thought JT loved her. But even while she carried their child in her belly, he had started having an affair. JT had destroyed her faith in humanity, and she really didn't know how she would ever get that back.

CHAPTER 21

Elder Unders was behind the podium beginning his sermon when Cassandra and JT walked into the sanctuary through the side door. Betty had held two seats for them in the front row. JT didn't want to attempt climbing the stairs to the pulpit area since he was still using his cane. As JT and Cassandra sat down, Elder Unders told the congregation that the title of his message was, "Don't Be Deceived." His subtitle was, "Be Careful When You Think You Stand, Lest You Fall."

Unders read from Matthews 12:25:

> *Every kingdom divided against itself is brought to desolation; and every city or house divided against itself shall not stand.*

JT squirmed a little in his seat as he thought about how long he had been divided against himself. For years now he had stood behind that podium and preached a hollow Word. He'd tried to encourage his members to live for God, when he wasn't really sure what that meant. Because if he had been sure what living for God really meant, how could he have destroyed his family and humiliated his wife the way he had?

He turned to Cassandra. As far as JT was concerned she was more beautiful now than the day he married her. He wanted her to forgive him, but really had no right to ask. Still, JT leaned over and said, "Thanks for bringing me to church."

Still looking toward the podium, she whispered, "I wanted to come myself, so it's no problem." She hadn't been to church since Diane Benson told her she had a baby by JT.

JT wanted to say more but he didn't want to stop Cassandra from soaking up as much of the Word as possible. JT himself needed as much of the Word as he could get, but he was feeling as if a bullseye was on his head. Every time Unders talked about believers being deceived concerning their relationship with the Lord, JT felt hundreds of eyes on him, as if the entire congregation knew of his transgressions. JT began to wonder if Unders had been led by the Lord to preach this message, or if he only decided to preach about being deceived once he knew that JT would be in service?

Unders looked out at the congregation and said, "Turn in your Bibles to Matthew 8:21–23. I want to show you how your deception doesn't deceive the Lord. He knows where you are, even when you don't." Unders lowered his head and began to read:

> *Not every one that saith unto me, Lord, Lord, shall enter into the kingdom of heaven; but he that doeth the will of my father which is in heaven.*
> *Many will say to me in that day, Lord, Lord, have we not prophesied in thy name, and in thy name*

*have cast out devils, and in thy name done many
wonderful works?*

*And then will I profess unto them, I never knew
you: depart from me, ye that work iniquity.*

Unders looked up from the Bible and asked, "Now, do
you really want to sit in church for years upon years, just
to hear the Lord tell you that He doesn't even know who
you are?"

That question haunted JT all through service and all the
way home. He sat in the kitchen with Cassandra and
asked her, "Do you think people can change?"

Cassandra sighed. "I've wondered the same thing myself, JT. But to be honest with you, I just don't know."

"Yeah, that's kind of how I feel about it." He shook his
head as he tried to explain everything he'd been feeling
these past few weeks. "I know I want to change. But I'm
so worried that I'll start off right, but then something will
happen to turn me back the wrong way again. What Unders said today at church stuck with me." He looked up at
Cassandra and said, "I don't want God to disown me. I
mean, it feels as if He already has. But I keep thinking
about King David and how he had disappointed God."

"But before it was all over, David had found favor with
God again," Cassandra said as she stood up and went to
the refrigerator. She opened it and then looked back at
JT and asked, "You want something to drink?"

"Do we have any Pepsi?"

She looked through the refrigerator and then told him,
"I don't think I bought Pepsi the last time I went to the
store. We have Sprite and fruit punch."

"I'll take some fruit punch," JT said.

Cassandra poured them both some fruit punch, grabbed
the pretzels off the counter and came back to the table.

"So what's up, JT? What are you trying to say?" she asked as she sat back down.

JT tapped his fingers on the table. He bit on his lip as he thought about Cassandra's question. He didn't want to just throw something out there. He decided that he wouldn't answer with his head, but his heart. He opened his mouth and told her, "I want to be right."

"Don't you think that's kind of ambiguous?"

Still tapping his fingers on the table he said, "The way I see it, if I'm right, as in, right with God, then I will be right with you and my sons. I would even be right with my church."

Cassandra put her hand over JT's to stop him from tapping. "I know it bothered you when the members of the church avoided us after service today. But I don't think they were trying to be unkind to you. I just think they didn't know what to say to us."

"I know that," he said softly. "They're uncomfortable with me because of all the things they are hearing. But I never wanted to make my own congregation uncomfortable. I didn't set out to do this, Sanni—I mean, Cassandra."

"Just look at it as another fence that needs mending," Cassandra told him.

"What about you, Cassandra? Do you think we could ever mend our relationship?"

Before she could answer, the telephone rang. Cassandra picked up the phone and said, "Hello."

"Let me speak to JT," the woman on the other end demanded.

"Who's calling?" Cassandra asked in as polite a tone as she could muster for any woman demanding to speak to her husband.

"You know who I am. Don't try to act like you don't know my voice."

"You've got about a second to tell me who this is, or I'm hanging up the phone," Cassandra told the caller.

"Oh, well if it's like that, I'll tell you who I am. This is the mother of JT's youngest child. Now can I please speak to my baby's daddy?" the woman said.

"Diane?"

"I thought you didn't know who I was." Diane said.

"Look, don't call my house—"

JT raised his hand to take the phone. "Let me handle this, Cassandra. I know why she's calling."

Reluctantly, Cassandra passed the telephone to JT, but she didn't move out of her seat.

"What is it, Diane?" JT asked.

"You know why I'm calling. Joe just brought these court papers over to me. Why couldn't you pick up the phone and tell me yourself that you wanted a paternity test?"

"I've been trying to recuperate from my accident, so I haven't been on the telephone much at all. The only address I had for you is Deacon Joe Benson's house, so that's where my attorney sent the paperwork. I trust that you will bring the baby to the hospital lab on Wednesday for the test?"

"I don't have nothing to hide, JT. Me and *your* baby will be there. So, you might as well tell Cassandra to get use to the idea of having another baby in the family," she said, then hung up.

He hung up the telephone and looked at Cassandra with a sheepish look on his face. "I'm sorry you had to go through that with Diane. But this will all be over soon. My attorney scheduled the paternity test for Wednesday."

"Why didn't you tell me?" she asked suspiciously.

"Honestly, I didn't want to bring it up before I needed to be there. I was thinking about telling you right before we had to go."

"That's just more deception wouldn't you say?" Cassandra asked.

"I just didn't want you to deal with this any sooner than necessary."

"Thanks for always thinking of what's best for me," Cassandra said snidely.

JT pointed at her. "See, that's exactly why I wanted to wait. I didn't want you walking around the house mad for a whole week. But Diane had to call here and spoil everything. That woman is nothing but a troublemaker."

"Oh, okay, I got you. It's Diane's fault that you slept with her," Cassandra said as she got up from the table and stomped out of the kitchen.

Cassandra hadn't spoken to JT in two days. And the only reason she spoke to him on the third day was because of the woman ringing her doorbell like a lunatic at six in the morning. While putting on her robe to go see who was at the door, Cassandra heard a woman screaming, "I'm not leaving, so you might as well open up this door." Then the woman started banging on the front door with her fist.

Cassandra ran down the stairs. However, JT had beaten her to the door. He swung it open and Cassandra saw Diane standing on the porch with a baby in her hands. She stopped midway down the stairs. She was stuck, couldn't move.

JT said to Diana, "Why are you at my house acting like a crazy woman?"

Diane did the sista-sista neck roll as she said, "Why aren't you answering your phone? Y'all over here living large while I'm staying with my sister in the ghetto."

"Nobody told you to leave your husband, Diane. You can't blame me for this."

Diane started screaming at him. "You haven't offered

me any money, bought any diapers; nothing. I'm not putting up with this mess." Diane pushed the baby in JT's chest. "Here, take your baby. I've got my own kids to raise."

JT had the cane in his hand. He dropped it so that he could put his arm around the baby. "Why are you doing this, Diane? We have the DNA test scheduled for today. Why don't you just let us find out who this baby's father is before you start bringing her to my house?"

Cassandra walked down the rest of the stairs and stood in front of the door to challenge Diane. "You can't leave this baby here."

"Oh, yes I can," Diane said, hands on hips. "I didn't lie down and make this baby on my own, and I'm not going to be a fool and take care of her on my own."

Cassandra turned to JT and said, "You can't let her do this. I can't take care of you, our kids, and this woman's child, too."

JT was struggling to hold the baby. He tried to switch her to the arm that had the cast, but he wasn't steady enough. He almost dropped her. Cassandra looked at Diane. The woman didn't even move to grab her baby. Cassandra took the child out of JT's arm and held her. She looked back at Diane with daggers in her eyes and said, "Is this what you want, Diane; another woman raising your child?"

"Hey, get used to it. Because if you stay with JT, you're going to be raising a bunch of children that you didn't give birth to," Diane said as she turned and walked away from them.

JT picked up his cane and followed Diane down the path toward the driveway. "Look, Diane, this is not right. You can't leave your baby on us. I won't stand for it."

Diane opened her car door, pulled out the diaper bag and handed it to JT. "I no longer care what you want, JT. You showed me what you were all about when you wouldn't even come see your own baby."

"Stop saying that. She's not my baby!"

Diane got in her car and started it. She rolled the window down and said, "She needs a bottle, so rush on back into the house and feed your baby." She drove off without looking back.

JT hung his head as he walked back into the house. He closed the door and looked at Cassandra with guilt-ridden eyes. Cassandra wanted to hit him, but she was holding the baby and no matter how mad she was at JT, she wouldn't harm an innocent child. "What are we supposed to do, JT?"

"I don't know, Cassandra." He swiped his hand over his head and then asked, "Do you think we can keep her until we get the DNA test results back?"

"I'm hanging on by a thread right now. I don't know how much more I can take," Cassandra told him as she walked away, shaking her head.

CHAPTER 22

Cassandra took the basinet and playpen out of the garage. She set up the basinet in her bedroom and the playpen in the family room. Aaron was using eight-ounce bottles now, so she took the four-ounce bottles she had put away out of the cabinet, boiled them, and then filled them with some of Aaron's baby formula. Her heart was heavy through it all. But Cassandra could no more mistreat this child than she could her own. She still remembered how she felt as a child when Bishop Turner's wife, Susan, treated her like an intruder.

Cassandra still didn't understand why her mother allowed Bishop to pick her up once a month for weekend visits. Bishop was her godfather, and she loved him for everything he'd done for her. But she really could have done without those weekend visits. Susan seemed angry every time she saw her. Cassandra had to admit though, as time went on and she grew up, her relationship with Susan improved, but she still never forgot feeling unwanted whenever she was in Susan's presence.

A baby started crying. Cassandra didn't know if it was

Lily or Aaron. But, one thing was for sure, both of them would be crying by the time she reached them. So she grabbed both an eight-ounce and a four-ounce bottle and ran up the stairs.

Just as she thought, Aaron sat up in his crib screaming his head off, while Lily wailed from her basinet. She gave Aaron his bottle and laid him back down in his crib, hoping he would cooperate. Then she walked over to the basinet, picked Lily up, and rocked her in her arms while giving her a bottle. Cassandra smiled as she looked down at the beautiful little girl in her arms. Looking at Lily made Cassandra think of Sarah. It hurt for a moment and a tear slid down her face. The nipple fell out of Lily's mouth and she began to cry again. Cassandra put the bottle back in her mouth and sang, "There's a Lily in the valley, and you're bright as the morning star."

Jerome picked that moment to run upstairs and yell, "Mom, Dad said we need to go to the hospital."

Aaron then popped back up, crying and holding out his arms for Cassandra. Lily turned her head from the bottle and also started screaming again. By the time Cassandra and the children were all ready to go to the hospital and take the DNA test, Cassandra was ready to scream herself. She'd had enough.

JT was in his room listening to one of his gospel CDs and reading his Bible. He was looking up verses on forgiveness because he found himself growing angry with Diane for disrupting his house and getting Cassandra so upset that she refused to even speak to him. But JT had to admit that he had no right to be angry with Diane. He was a married man when Diane approached him, and if he didn't want drama in his life, then he should have told her to keep stepping. But he hadn't done that. He'd reveled in his sins. Now he was reading his Word and trying to find a way to forgive Diane. Truth be told, JT was also trying to forgive himself. He closed his Bible and was getting ready to pray when there was a knock on his door. "Come in," he said as he put his Bible on the table next to his chair.

Cassandra walked into his room. She stood with her back against the wall. JT asked, "Is everyone ready to go?"

"Yes, but I need to talk to you first." Her face was set as she said, "I've tried to help you get through this time of healing. But then one of your women left a dead rat on my doorstep and another left her baby for me to take care of; I'm done."

He tried to stop her from finishing what she was saying. He held up his hand. "Don't say it, Cassandra."

She took a deep breath and said, "I want a divorce."

"Baby," JT said as he stood up and walked toward her.

She was still leaning against the wall, but tears were flowing down her face. She shook her head. "I don't want to be with you anymore."

JT was standing in front of her now. He wished he had the use of both arms so he could wipe the tears from both her cheeks at one time. But he made due with the one arm he had the use of and wiped away her tears. "Don't do this, Cassandra. You are the kindest person I know. And if Lily turns out to be my child, I know that you will grow to love her. Just give us a chance."

"Lily's not the problem, JT. Believe it or not, I care about that little girl already. And even if I didn't, I wouldn't mistreat her. The problem is you. I don't trust you, and I can't raise all these kids on my own."

"You won't have to. I'll help."

She smirked at that. "I've asked you to help me with the boys since I had them, but you never would. You said that's the reason I stay at home, to do everything for the kids. Well, I'm not going to do this anymore."

"I'm sorry. I'm not the same man who did all that stuff

to you. I don't know how to make you believe that, but I will spend the rest of my life trying, if you just give me the chance."

She moved his hand from her face. "It's too late, JT."

"What do you want me to do, Sanni?"

"I've asked you not to call me that. You haven't earned the right to be so personal with me."

His face was tortured as he told her, "I've lost so much already, Cassandra. I really don't want to lose you, too. I know it doesn't seem like it, but I want my family."

She pulled herself off the wall. Anger flared in her eyes. "You should have thought about that before you got another woman pregnant." She turned to walk out of his room, put her hand on the doorknob, then turned back to JT. "You can stay here while you look for another place to live, but I'd like you to move out within a month."

She walked out of his room, and JT didn't stop her. He looked to heaven and shook his head. He walked back to his bed and fell on his knees. The tears that flowed down Cassandra's face were nothing like the rain storm flowing down his face right now. He cried out to the Lord, "How much more, Lord? How much more?" He stretched out on the floor and poured out his heart to God.

"This hurts, Lord. But if this is what I have to go through to grow in faith, then continue to purge me. Please create in me a clean heart. I just want to be right, God. So, do what You have to do to me, but help me. I can take losing everything else, Lord. But I can't take losing You or my family. Please help Cassandra find forgiveness in her heart." When he was finished praying, he got off the floor and left the house with his family so he could take a paternity test.

CHAPTER 23

Just as JT had suspected, the rest of the week was a nightmare. Handling all three kids was too much for Cassandra. JT wasn't much help since he only had the use of one arm. So after they went to the hospital to take the DNA test, Cassandra called her mother for help. Mattie arrived at their house within thirty minutes with three suitcases. She pushed the door open, sighed, and then said, "Whew, baby girl, I got here as fast as I could. I told you not to marry that lowlife. Didn't I tell you?"

JT was in the entryway with Cassandra when his mother-in-law came in. He gave her a crooked smile and said, "I love you too, mother-in-law."

Mattie scrunched her nose as if she'd smelled a dead rat covered in sour milk. "I don't like the sound of that. I hope you won't be able to call me mother-in-law for very long."

"Okay, Mom, now I asked for your help. But please don't start," Cassandra said.

Jerome ran to Mattie and hugged her. "Grandma, Grandma, you're here."

"Hey, scooter. Of course I'm here. I had to come see about you, didn't I?" she said as she bent to hug her grandson.

JT pulled Cassandra aside and asked, "How long does your mom think she's staying here?"

Cassandra rolled her eyes and walked away from him, shaking her head. JT observed that Cassandra had been shaking her head at him a lot lately. He couldn't wait to get the results of the test. He hoped that he and Cassandra would be able to move on with their lives once they received the results, but the way Cassandra was acting, JT didn't even know if she would still be in the house each morning when he awoke. He kept expecting to find her closet empty with a note saying that she and the boys had gone to her mother's house. But, of course, Cassandra had told him to get out, so he guessed that Mattie had moved in for good.

Mattie took care of Lily so that Cassandra didn't have to do it all. But the following week, when the cast came off his arm, Mattie brought the baby to his room and said, "Guess what, preacher man? You gon' be taking care of your own child from this point on."

"Look, Mattie, don't open my door without knocking on it first," JT told her.

"Boy, you just take this baby. Her diaper needs to be changed."

JT said, "Can you take her to Cassandra?"

Mattie forcefully put Lily in his arms, dropped the diaper bag at his feet, and said, "I wish I would." She wagged her finger at him. "You are a real lowlife. I wish my daughter had never laid eyes on you."

He lowered his head in shame. "I'm sorry. You're right. I should change her diaper myself," JT admitted.

Mattie harrumphed. "You gon' be doing more than that for yourself. Cassandra is finally coming to her senses about you. Now that you've got that cast off your arm, you will be out of here soon."

JT laid Lily on his bed and was in the process of changing her diaper while Mattie was on her tirade. He turned toward his mother-in-law and asked, "Why are you so hateful?"

" 'Cause I can't stand jack-legged preachers like you; thinking you rule the world. But you ain't worth the time it took your mama to push you out." She left his room after making that remark.

JT's eyes rolled heavenward. His mother-in-law really tested his salvation. He knew one thing for sure: if he could make it through a conversation with Mattie Daniels without cursing her out, he must be crawling his way back to God. Lily let out a small cry. JT sat down in his chair and rocked her. This was the first time since Lily had been in his home that he'd actually made time for her. Looking in her face, JT wondered if this child could really be his. She didn't look like his other kids, but did that really matter?

His bedroom door opened again as Mattie brought Lily's basinet into his room. "She's going to sleep in here with you from now on." Mattie laughed as she added, "Enjoy yourself, because this baby wakes up about three times a night."

JT tried the high road approach with Mattie. "Thank you for helping us out with her. I've been trying to reach her mother so that she can pick Lily up, but I haven't had any success."

Mattie laughed at him again. "Cassandra didn't tell you?"

"Tell me what?"

"Diane dropped off her other three children with Deacon Benson and left town. She's starting a new life in a new city, or so she said."

JT started stuttering. "B—but she can't do that. She can't just leave us with her child."

Mattie put her hands on her hips as she said, "Let's get one thing straight, Mr. Adultery Committing Pastor, Diane didn't leave nothing on *us*. She left this baby on you. And you are the only somebody who's responsible for taking care of her."

"If this baby is proven not to be mine, then Cassandra doesn't have to worry about helping me take care of her."

Smirking, Mattie said, "You can save that for somebody else. I know all about you, "my wife doesn't understand my ministry" type of pastors, and I'm sorry I ever let that jack-leg bishop talk Cassandra into marrying the likes of you." Her eyes bore into him with contempt as she walked out of his room and closed the door behind her.

JT felt unwanted in his own house. He wanted to stay in his room and not bother anyone for the rest of the day. But Lily needed a bottle. He walked out of his bedroom and headed toward the kitchen to get one. He heard Cassandra and Mattie talking and stopped to listen.

Mattie said, "When are you going to get some sense in your head and realize that dog ain't about to change?"

"He's different, Mama," Cassandra said.

"He's holding his breath. What do you think; that he's going to act like the dog he is, when he knows he needs you? No, he's waiting until his luck changes. But you mark my word, girl. As soon as things are looking up for him, he is going to show out on you all over again."

"I'm not saying that I'm going to stay married to JT. I'm just saying I see a different man these days. He's been humbled in ways I don't even think he realizes," Cassandra said.

"Yeah, well, you keep philosophizing and you're going to have a house full of humble children from wayward women to take care of."

"That's not fair, Mother. You act like you think I'm stupid."

"I don't think you're stupid," Mattie said. "You've got a big heart. You were always like this, even when you were a kid. I still remember all those stray dogs you brought home and loved and cared for until we found a home for them. But, Cassandra, honey, the dog you have now don't need your love. He needs a swift kick."

As JT listened to his wife, his heart lifted a bit. He understood why she wouldn't want him as a husband anymore; he hoped to change her mind, but he understood. But what lifted his heart was the fact that Cassandra had noticed a change in him. Not wanting to hear anymore of Mattie's insults, JT walked into the kitchen and greeted everyone. Cassandra was seated at the table feeding the boys. Mattie was at the sink washing dishes.

Cassandra said, "Good morning, JT. How is Miss 'Sleep As Little As Possible' doing?"

He smiled at Cassandra's joke as he looked at the baby in his arms. "Right now she wants a bottle." He looked at his boys and asked, "Do you need me to do anything for you or the boys?"

"No, but it looks like you need me to hold Lily while you get her bottle." Cassandra took the baby out of JT's arms.

JT saw Mattie roll her eyes, but he ignored her as he asked, "Does she have any bottles ready?"

Cassandra pointed. "They're in the fridge, but you need to warm it in hot water before giving it to Lily."

"Okay, thanks," JT said as he took a bottle out of the refrigerator. Mattie handed him a pot with water in it. At first JT thought she was going to throw the contents of the pot on him, so he jumped back.

Mattie laughed wickedly and said, "Boy, put that bottle in this pot."

"Thank you," he said, feeling stupid for assuming she was trying to scald him with a pot of hot grits or something. He turned on the stove and then turned back to Cassandra. "What are you and the boys planning to do today?"

"I'm getting ready to take the boys into the family room and let them watch a few educational cartoons," Cassandra told him.

"Do you mind if Lily and I join you?"

Cassandra looked at JT but didn't answer.

He got the message and backed off. "Hey, I wasn't trying to crowd you. I just thought we could spend some time with the boys together."

"You know what, JT?" Cassandra said with a smile on her face, "you are more than welcome to spend time with the boys this morning. If you want to pick out the DVDs while I finish feeding them breakfast, that would be great."

"Thanks, Cassandra," JT said as he walked out of the kitchen in search of the DVDs for his sons.

JT hadn't put more than a foot outside of the kitchen when he heard Mattie say, "Don't be a fool, Cassandra. You gon' regret giving that devil an inch."

He wanted to turn around and plead his case. He needed Cassandra to believe that he would never take her for granted again. But how could he convince her of something like that while she was holding proof positive of a situation that should have never happened? He kept walking, went into the family room, and looked through the DVDs. Cassandra was really good about making sure the kids participated in learning activities. She purchased all sorts of learning tools for the kids. He found a *Heroes of the Bible* DVD and pulled it out. He also pulled out a *Dora the Explorer* learning DVD. He then went back to the kitchen to take Lily's bottle out of the pot, but Mattie already had the bottle in her hand.

When he walked into the kitchen, Mattie said, "Leave it to you and I guess you would give this baby scalding hot milk."

He really wanted to tell this woman to shut up, but he was already in hot water with his wife. He wouldn't win any points with Cassandra by telling her mother off. He bit his lip as he turned to Cassandra. "I pulled out a couple of DVDs. We're ready to go whenever you are."

Vivian stood in the Thomases backyard, peeping through the family room window. The family looked happy as they sat around the family room, laughing, joking, and watching a bunch of stupid cartoons. Vivian wanted to throw a brick through the window. She would love to see JT's face as the brick sailed through the window and landed smack dab in the middle of Cassandra's fat head.

JT would be horrified to see his precious Cassandra with a big brick dent in her head. Vivian laughed at the image. But then she remembered that she was peeking through their blinds, and ducked. She got on her knees and crawled all the way back to the front of the house, and then ran to her car, where she saw the spray paint can in the passenger seat. "There you are," she said.

She picked up the can and got back out of her car. When she had been in the backyard being a peeper, she had wondered if she'd left the spray paint at home. She had been angry with herself, thinking that she'd missed an opportunity. She walked right up to the front door and spelled out "s-i-n-n-e-r." The front door was tan, the spray paint, red, so the letters were much more magnified for all the neighbors to read.

Vivian dropped the can in the yard as she ran back to

her car. As she sped off, Vivian's visual picture of the scene in the family room caused her to pull over the car and think about what she had seen. Cassandra was on the couch with Jerome. JT was on the floor with Aaron. But there was also a baby in the playpen. She knew this because the baby cried every so often and JT would get up and tend to the baby.

"Why did JT tend to the baby every time it cried? If Cassandra was babysitting for someone, wouldn't she have gotten up to see about the baby?"

When Vivian was sixteen, her mother made her give her baby up for adoption. All these years she'd thought that her baby was gone for good. At least, that's what her therapist had told her. But that hack didn't know insane from sane, that's why Vivian stopped going to her sessions. And now look; things were finally turning around for her. She had known all along that fate had brought her and JT together, and now she knew why. JT had been keeping her baby for her. As she put her car in drive and continued on her journey, Vivian wondered why her baby hadn't gotten any bigger in all these years. But then she decided not to trouble her mind with insignificant details. She had bigger things to think about, like how she would get her baby away from JT.

CHAPTER 24

"I want that woman arrested, I'm tired of this!" JT yelled at the police officer as they stood in the front yard looking at his door.

"Did you see this woman anywhere near your house today?" the police officer asked.

"No, we were in the house all day. We didn't even know she had spray painted my house until my neighbor rang the door bell and told me."

"I will check into this, Mr. Thomas. But I can't arrest her without an eye witness."

JT looked at the man's badge and then said, "Look, Grayson, my primary concern is my family. Vivian is obviously unstable—she slashed my tires, left a dead rat on my doorstep, and now she's spray painting my house. What more do you want this psychotic woman to do to my family before you take action?"

Grayson looked at his notes and then told JT, "One good thing is that she was in front of your house the day you found the dead rat. So, I should be able to question her on that with no problem. The rest is a little shaky, but I will do my best."

JT rubbed his forehead and around his eyes, making circular motions with his hands on his face. He took a deep breath and then exhaled. "Okay, Detective, you do what you can and I'll protect my family the best way I can."

"Be careful," Grayson said as he walked away.

JT was fuming as he went back into the house. Cassandra and Mattie were waiting in the living room for him. The kids had been put down for their afternoon nap. "What did he say?" Cassandra asked as soon as JT walked into the living room.

"Not much they can do." JT angrily shook his head. "I don't understand this. Vivian comes over here and terrorizes my family and the police can't do anything because she didn't sign her artwork."

"Are they going to question her about this stuff?" Cassandra wanted to know.

"Yes, but that's about it." JT sat down across from Cassandra and said, "I'm really getting tired of this."

"Well, if that's the case, maybe you won't be pulling your pants down at anymore church functions," Mattie said with a raised eyebrow.

JT exploded. He shot up and pointed at Mattie. "I want you out of my house today. Get your bags and get out of here." He'd taken all he was going to take from this woman.

Undaunted, Mattie stood up and told JT, "You wish this was your house. When my daughter gets finished taking you to the bank, you'll be sleeping in your car."

"Mother," Cassandra said while raising her hand to quiet the situation.

"Don't *mother* me," Mattie said as she turned to her

daughter. "Why do you let this lowlife get away with treating you like dirt? I'm sick of it. Do you hear me?" Mattie was becoming hysterical as she continued. "I saw how you were acting toward JT in the family room today. And you didn't look like no woman planning to see her divorce attorney. I won't let him treat you like this. Do you hear me?"

"Mother, calm down," Cassandra said as she walked over to her hyperventilating mother, grabbed hold of her arm, and sat her back on the couch. "Why are you acting like this? What's wrong?"

"He's no good, baby. Them preachers are no good, the whole lot of 'em," Mattie said.

"That's not true, Mother, there are some good men out there who preach the Gospel. You can't look at my situation and lump all the preachers in the world."

JT stood in his living room amazed at this woman's hatred. He knew where her hatred came from. It was a secret he had kept for all the years he'd know Cassandra. But he couldn't hold it any longer. He had to let Cassandra know what was going on before her mother's bitterness became a cancer to her also. He put his hand on Cassandra's shoulder and said, "Baby, your mother feels this way about preachers because your father is a preacher."

Cassandra swung around to face her husband. "What are you talking about, JT? My father was a soldier. He died in the Vietnam war." She turned back to her mother looking for confirmation and said, "Right, Mother?"

Mattie patted Cassandra's hand as she kept her eyes averted from JT and said, "Yes, honey, your daddy was a soldier. I still miss him to this day."

"Tell her the truth," JT demanded.

Eyes of hatred looked up at JT. "What do you know about it? You weren't there."

"Yeah, but I can see, Mattie. And I asked questions about what I saw and, low and behold, I found out I was right. You have lied to Cassandra for years and have afflicted her with your hate because of something you did."

With a raised eyebrow, Cassandra asked, "What is it that you see, JT?"

JT put his hands on both of Cassandra's shoulders as he faced her. "Don't you see it, baby? The two of you have the same bone structure and your eyes are exactly alike. Sometimes when I've looked into your eyes, it was as if he were standing right there with us."

Cassandra sat down as her eyes filled with revelation. She put her hand to her mouth and lowered her head for a moment. When she raised her head back up, she looked at her mother and said, "Do you remember when I was six years old and I came home from a weekend at Bishop's house?"

Mattie nodded but said nothing.

"I told you that Troy said his mom told Bishop she was tired of his illegitimate child coming over their house. Troy told me that they were talking about me, so I asked you what an illegitimate child was and do you remember what you said?"

Again, Mattie nodded but said nothing.

Cassandra wasn't letting her off the hook though. "You said that an illegitimate child is one who lost her father, and another nice father steps in to take his place. You told me that mean old Susan was just angry about how special I was to Bishop."

JT looked at Mattie. He saw her eyes fill with tears, and at that moment he actually felt sorry for the woman. He could see by the pain etched on her face that she still felt guilty for what she had done all those years ago. He sat down next to Cassandra and said, "Everyone makes mistakes, baby. We've just got to learn from them and move on."

But Cassandra wasn't listening. Her jaw was set tight as her eyes bore through her mother. "Is Bishop Turner my father?"

Mattie sat silently with her head lowered and tears falling on her lap.

"Answer me!" Cassandra demanded.

"It's complicated, Cassandra," Mattie said finally.

"How complicated?" Cassandra asked in a tone that dared her mother not to respond.

"My husband was away at war, Cassandra. I was lonely, and when my husband died, I was so vulnerable that I fell into that awful man's arms and he never even apologized for how he took advantage of me," Mattie said as she stood up with her arms folded across her chest. "I'm leaving. I can see that I'm not wanted here and I will not stay where I'm not wanted." She grabbed her purse and began walking toward the door.

Before Mattie could walk through the door, Cassandra said, "You still didn't answer my question. Is Bishop Turner my father?"

Mattie opened the front door, she looked at the words that spelled out "sinner" and said, "Yes." Then she closed the door behind her and left.

As the door closed, Cassandra put her hands over her face and sobbed. JT sat back down next to Cassandra and pulled her close to him. "How could she . . . how could she?"

As much as JT wanted Cassandra to be mad at her mother so that she would draw closer to him, he couldn't do it. Cassandra loved her mother and she needed to remember that right now. "Your mom is human, just like we are. You need to give her a chance to explain all of this to you."

She pulled herself out of his arms and wiped the tears from her face. "Don't you take up for her. She doesn't even like you."

CHAPTER 25

Cassandra picked up her telephone and dialed Bishop's cell phone. It rang once and then he picked up. "Hey, sweetheart, how are you doing?"

Cassandra was hurt and angry. Tears were flowing down her face as she said, "How could you?"

"What? Cassandra, what's wrong?"

"How dare you? How could you make me believe that you were no more than my godfather all these years?"

Bishop stuttered. "W—what's going on?"

"You know what's going on. I know the truth and I will never forgive you for this."

"N—now wait a minute, sweetheart, I don't think you know the whole truth," Bishop said.

"Oh, I know," Cassandra told him, her voice steadily rising as she continued. "I know that you brought me to your house on weekends and allowed Susan to treat me like I was nothing. I always knew she didn't like me, I just never imagined that this was the reason."

"Stop crying, Cassandra. Susan loves you, honey. She's told you that more than once."

Cassandra wiped some of the tears from her face. "She treats me all right now. But when I was a kid, I could tell that she didn't like me. And that was because of what you had done—it was your fault."

"I'm coming to town today, Cassandra. I'll be there to see you this evening. I really want to talk to you about this," Bishop said.

"No, no." Cassandra waved her hands in the air. "I don't ever want to see you again." She slammed down the telephone.

The telephone immediately rang and Cassandra put her hands over her ears. She screamed as she walked around the living room. JT walked into the family room carrying Aaron on one hip and Lily on the other. "Why aren't you picking up the phone? I was changing diapers so I couldn't get it."

"It's Bishop, and I don't want to talk to him," Cassandra said, hands on hips.

"Calm down, Cassandra," JT said as he put Aaron in his playpen and laid Lily on the couch.

"What's wrong with Mommy?" Jerome asked.

JT turned the TV to *SpongeBob SquarePants* and said, "Sit down and watch TV, Jerome. Mommy is okay, I just need to talk to her."

As JT started walking toward Cassandra the telephone rang again. They both looked at it. She shook her head and turned away. JT picked up the phone. "Hello . . . Oh, how are you, Susan?" JT hesitated, and then said as he turned to Cassandra, "Can I have her call you back?" Another hesitation, then, "I understand, but Cassandra doesn't want to talk to any—"

Cassandra held out her hand. "Give me the phone."

He put his hand over the mouthpiece and asked, "Are you sure?"

"Yes, I want to talk to her," she said as JT put the cordless phone in her hand. Cassandra walked into the hallway and put the receiver to her ear. JT followed her into the hallway and stood there looking nervous. "Hi, Susan."

"Cassandra, honey, the bishop just called me. When he told me what you said, I had to give you a call," Susan said.

"I'm sorry this happened to you, Susan. My husband has just had a child by another woman, so I now know firsthand how awful something like that is."

When Cassandra made the remark about Lily, JT went back into the family room and sat down with the kids to get out of her line of fire.

"I wondered why you didn't seem to like me when I was a child. I kept trying to do things to make you like me, but now I understand."

"We may have started off rough, honey, but you made me love you. I need you to know that I truly love you. I wanted to tell you that Bishop is your father so long ago, but we'd kept up this charade for too long."

"How can you forgive Bishop for doing this to you?"

"It wasn't easy. We fought for years after he admitted his mistake to me. But I love him. He's the only man I've ever wanted to be with. So we worked it out," Susan told her.

Cassandra glanced toward the family room, where JT sat with his extracurricular baby, and said, "I don't know if I can work this out."

"Give him a chance, Cassandra. From what the bishop has told me, JT has been through a lot lately. God may have humbled and changed him."

"I've got to go, but I do want you to know that I am truly sorry for what my mother and Bishop did to you."

"And I want to let you know that I'm glad you were born. You are the daughter I never had."

Cassandra hung up the phone and walked back into the

family room. She sat down on the couch next to Lily. As she looked at this little baby, she wondered if someday she would come to think of Lily as the daughter she didn't give birth to. Or would she only think of her as JT's betrayal?

"Are you okay?" JT asked.

"No, I'm anything but okay," she told him.

JT turned to Jerome. "Hey, little man, why don't you go get some of your trucks and toy men so we can play together?"

Jerome jumped up. "Okay, Dad. I'll be right back."

As Jerome ran out of the room, JT turned back to Cassandra and said, "I'm sorry, baby. I just thought it was time that you knew the truth."

"I bet you did," Cassandra said, glaring at JT. "I guess you thought that if I knew my own mother did the same thing that Diane has done to me; if I knew that I am the child of an affair, I would just shut up about what you did, huh?"

"That's not what I was thinking, Cassandra."

She stood up. "You probably even asked Susan to call me. I bet you thought after Susan told me she stayed with Bishop because he had changed, you hoped that I would stay with you. But I don't know if I can do this." She pointed to Lily and continued, "I don't ever want to treat her like an inconvenient intrusion. That's how I felt growing up. Susan doesn't treat me that way now, but it took her twenty years to treat me like I was a human being with feelings that mattered." Tears started back down her face. "I can't do that to Lily, JT."

JT went to his wife and pulled her into his arms. "I don't know how to say this in a way that you will believe, but I am so sorry for what I did to our family."

She pulled away from JT and said, "I've got to get out of here."

"Where are you going?"

"I need to think, and I can't stay here to do that." She looked around the room at the three children and felt guilty for leaving JT alone with all of them. "Look, I'll take Aaron with me so you don't have to deal with all three of them by yourself."

"I know I have no right to ask this, but would you take Lily instead?"

Cassandra looked at JT as if he had lost his mind. After a moment, she recovered enough to ask, "Why would I do that?"

"See," JT began, wringing his hands, "I think you have a big enough heart to treat Lily just as good as you treat our children, but you're not sure. So, if you had some time alone with Lily, maybe you would realize what I already know."

She thought about that for a moment, then realized that she would like to know how she would feel about Lily when it was just the two of them. She didn't answer JT, but she walked into the garage and came back to the family room with the infant car seat that had been replaced months ago with Aaron's toddler car seat. "Put this in my car and I'll get her diaper bag ready."

Vivian had come up with a plan to get her baby back. She rented a car just in case JT had given the police the license plate number, make, and model of her car. The car's windows were also tinted, but not so tinted that she couldn't see that a piece of cardboard now covered the red letters she had spray painted on that door. She passed the house, and then parked her car two doors down. She had on a blond wig and an extra bulky sweat suit. So Vivian figured if neighbors were looking out the window, they wouldn't be able to describe her correctly to the police. She walked down the street with purpose. As far as Vivian was concerned, JT had no business covering up her handy work. She wanted everyone to know that he was a sinner and she was going to rip that cardboard off the door. She stopped in her tracks as JT's front door opened. Cassandra walked out the door carrying a baby that was too small to be Aaron.

She watched Cassandra put the baby in a car seat. She threw the diaper bag in the backseat and closed the door. Vivian ran back to her car. She got behind the wheel and started the car. Her adrenaline was pumping as she watched Cassandra drive by. Now Vivian was angry. Not only was JT keeping her baby away from her, but he had obviously given her to Cassandra. Something had to be done to stop them. Vivian followed the woman who'd taken her man and now her baby.

CHAPTER 26

Lily cooed in the back as Cassandra drove down the street. Cassandra adjusted her rearview mirror so she could see Lily. The child was blowing bubbles, too. She looked adorable. "So, where do you want to go, Lily?"

Lily's response was to blow another bubble.

Cassandra laughed. "Did you say mall? Don't tell me that you're already wanting to shop? Okay, off to the mall we'll go. Maybe we'll find you a few outfits. What do you think about that?"

Cassandra righted the rearview mirror and continued driving. As she drove, she thought about Susan Turner. The woman had been so awful to her when she was a child. Cassandra didn't understand how a Christian could claim to love God and mistreat an innocent child. But Cassandra also wondered how she could claim to love God and not forgive Susan. She actually thought she had forgiven Susan, but when she discovered that Bishop was actually her father, all of her childhood pain came rushing back into her adult life, and she felt vulnerable again.

She had grown up wanting to be loved so badly that she

fell into one man's arms after another. Her heart had gotten tangled up into so many bad relationships that Cassandra thought she would die if she didn't find relief. That's when Bishop prayed with her and helped guide her closer to God. Cassandra was so thankful for Bishop's wisdom, and she always knew he had her best interests at heart, so when he introduced her to JT, Cassandra thought JT would be the man for her.

She didn't question the fact that JT loved her when they first married, but she did notice the change in him after their first child died. JT had recently explained his changing behavior by telling her he had stopped trusting God. That lack of trust in God had evidently caused him to loosen his morals, and then cheating on her became easy. Cassandra wondered if that was how other Christians went astray. God doesn't come through on some issue deemed all important, so the sold-out Christian does the backstroke, and moves as far away from God as possible.

As she parked the car in the mall lot, Cassandra prayed that God would heal her heart. She took the stroller out of the trunk and put Lily in it. "Well, young lady, let's go run up these credit cards," Cassandra said with a laugh as she pushed the stroller inside the mall.

Cassandra and Lily went into The Children's Place, Macy's, Baby Gap and JCPenney. It was truly a girls' day out, and they were putting a hurting on the Visa card. Then Lily started crying. Cassandra bent down to check on her. "What's wrong?" she asked, as if a three-month-old baby could answer her question. "I bet you're hungry." Cassandra sat down in the food court, took a bottle out of the diaper bag, and fed Lily.

When Lily was done drinking the bottle, Cassandra burped her, and took her into the bathroom to change her diaper. Her cell phone started ringing just as she finished changing Lily's diaper. Cassandra pulled her phone out of her purse and answered it.

"Hey, how are things going?" JT asked.

"We're doing just fine. What's up?" Cassandra asked as she picked Lily up off the changing table.

"I was just checking on you."

"Okay," Cassandra said with a raised eyebrow and a roll of the eyes.

"Where are you?"

We're at the mall, okay? Now can I talk to you when I get home?"

"Oh, sure," JT said. Then after hesitating for a moment he asked, "Do you think you could stop and pick up a couple of burgers for me and Jerome?"

"Sure, JT. I'll see you all in a little bit." She hit the end button, and then put the phone back in her purse.

"Let's go," she said as she put Lily back in the stroller and headed out of the mall. As she pushed the stroller toward the car, Cassandra wondered if there was such a thing as forgiveness? As a Christian, she heard people talk about forgiving others all the time. But now that she had experienced hurt and betrayal on every front, and she had such a long line of people that she needed to forgive, Cassandra didn't know if she could do it.

When they reached the car, Cassandra took Lily out of the stroller, put her in the car seat, and latched it. She opened the trunk and threw their bags in. She folded the stroller and tucked it in next to the bags. Just as she was about to close the trunk, she felt the point of something digging in her back.

"Turn around," a woman said.

As Cassandra put her hands in the air, she told her assailant, "I have money and credit cards in my purse. They're yours, but please don't hurt us."

"I don't want your money."

Cassandra turned around and looked right into Vivian Sampson's hate-filled face. As she lowered her eyes, she saw the knife in Vivian's hand. Her eyes widened with fear as she asked, "What do you want?"

"I want you and JT to stop acting like you're this perfect couple, when everybody knows nothing could be further from the truth."

"Well, you've got your wish, we are far from perfect. Now, can you please leave us alone?"

"The whole church is going to know when I'm through with the two of you," Vivian said as she lifted her knife and slashed it in Cassandra's direction. Cassandra jumped back as the blade slashed through her three-hundred-dollar Coach purse strap.

Cassandra looked around, hoping that someone would come into the parking lot and help her. But she had parked in the back of the mall. She liked this spot in the back because it was closer to the door, and there was always less traffic. So, consequently, no one was coming to her rescue. "What do you want? Why are you doing this?" Cassandra screamed at her.

Lily started crying. Cassandra tried to back up enough so that Lily could see her, but Vivian grabbed her arm and pushed her against the car. "Get away from her, she's mine."

Cassandra saw the wild look in Vivian's eyes, and knew that something had gone really wrong inside her head. She watched Vivian reach into the backseat and try to unhook Lily's car seat. At that moment, Cassandra was struck with the same maternal instinct she had for Jerome and Aaron. She was no longer tolerating this child simply because she was sweet and innocent. Her relationship with Lily had some how reached another level without Cassandra realizing it. She was willing to die to protect this child;

JT's child. She pulled Vivian away from Lily. "Don't you touch her," Cassandra yelled.

"No! No! She's mine," Vivian screamed as she lifted her arm and lashed out at Cassandra while still holding the knife.

She stabbed Cassandra three times before Cassandra fell to the ground. "Help us!" Cassandra yelled with all her might. Vivian leaned back into the car and snatched out the car seat. Cassandra pulled herself off the ground and tackled Vivian from behind still hollering, "Help! Help us!"

Vivian turned and jabbed Cassandra with her knife and then took off running with Lily. Cassandra couldn't move, couldn't breathe. She fell back down with her arms stretched out toward Lily. The last thing she said before slipping into unconsciousness was, "My baby."

JT, Jerome, and Aaron arrived at the hospital with Bishop, who had been at the house waiting for Cassandra to get home so he could explain himself. There would be no explaining done that night, however. The doctor came out of the operating room and informed JT that Cassandra was out of surgery, but unconscious.

Jerome stepped up to the doctor and asked, "What's wrong with my mommy?"

JT adjusted Aaron from his left hip to the right as he hurriedly asked the doctor, "When can I see her?"

"Give us a little while longer. I'll send someone out here to let you know when you can come back. But somebody was watching over your wife. One of the knife wounds was less than an inch away from puncturing her heart."

"Will she make it, Doctor?" Bishop asked.

"Only time will tell. We need to monitor her through the night and we'll have a better idea in the morning," the doctor said.

"What about Lily? Where is she?" JT asked.

"Who is Lily?"

"My daughter. She was with my wife," JT said.

"You might want to ask the woman in the waiting room," the doctor said, pointing to a woman in a blue denim dress.

JT noticed that the woman had Cassandra's purse on her lap as he walked into the waiting room.

She stood and asked him, "Are you Cassandra's husband?"

"Yes," he answered.

"I'm the lady who called you. Your wife's cell phone was in her purse and I just dialed the last incoming call. Thank God I reached you." She handed Cassandra's purse to JT. "I don't know if anything was stolen from this. I just took out her cell phone."

Betty ran down the hall toward them. A look of horror was etched across her face as she stood before them. "Thank you so much for calling me, Bishop." She then turned her attention to JT, gave him a hug and then asked, "How is she, Pastor?"

"Not good." His voice broke as he added, "She's unconscious right now."

Bishop turned to Betty and said, "I called you because we need your help."

"Anything, Bishop. Just let me know what I can do," Betty replied.

"I was hoping you would feel that way. JT and I might be out here all night, so I called to see if you could take the kids."

She took Aaron away from JT and said, "I'll take the kids. But please give me a call as soon as you know something about Cassandra."

JT was touched by the fact that Betty would still be so

kind to his family, even when she didn't have to be. Bishop had basically suspended him, and Betty was now taking her orders from Elder Unders. With this action, Betty was showing herself to not just be an employee of his, but a friend, and JT was humbled by that. He hugged Betty again as his eyes moistened. "Thank you, Betty. I can't tell you how much I appreciate what you are doing for us."

"It's not a problem, Pastor. I would do anything for you and your wife."

"How can you still call me that? I certainly don't deserve to be called pastor by anyone."

Betty put her hand on JT's shoulder and said, "You are what God says you are." She took the kids and left the hospital.

JT turned back to the woman who had looked out for Cassandra. "Thank you, for what you did for my wife. I just hope she survives this attack," JT said as he sat down and covered his face with his hands.

"I'm sorry I didn't get there in time to stop that woman from stealing the baby," the woman said.

JT lifted his head. "What happened? Please tell me what you saw."

"Okay," the woman said as began to tell her story. "I was coming out of the mall when I heard someone hollering for help. I ran toward the sound and saw your wife jump on this woman's back. She was fighting like a tiger, but the other woman must have turned and stabbed her, because she fell to the ground. When I reached your wife, I heard her say, 'My baby.' That's when I noticed that the woman was running away with a car seat. I'm so sorry; I couldn't get the baby because I had to get an ambulance for your wife. She was bleeding pretty badly."

Bishop put his hand on JT's shoulder as he said, "They are going to be all right. You've got to trust God on this."

This is where JT had stood before. He had lost a child and his faith in God. Now, with the possibility of losing his wife and another child, would he choose faith, or stumble and fall all over again? "Vivian did this. I just know she did."

"Did you hear me, JT?" Bishop asked when he didn't get a response.

With determination, JT nodded. "Yeah, I heard you. We've got to trust God on this one."

The police officer JT had spoken with earlier in the day when Vivian had spray painted his door walked over to him. "Mr. Thomas, we received the call at the precinct about your wife. Since I talked with you earlier, I decided to come out again."

JT was furious. How could the police send the same man who was at his house this afternoon? He didn't care about what Vivian had done to them this afternoon and JT doubted that he cared now. "I need to speak with someone else, Detective Grayson. My wife has been stabbed, my daughter is missing, and I'm just not convinced that you care all that much." It struck JT that he kept referring to Lily as his daughter. He hadn't received the DNA test back yet, but somehow JT knew in his heart that little girl was his child.

Detective Grayson lifted his hands to ward off JT's verbal assault. "Hold on, Mr. Thomas. I'm on your side here. Believe me, you don't know how sorry I am that my hands were tied earlier. I wish I could have stopped this. But I'm here to help now."

"You need to speak with the woman who saw the attack," Bishop told Detective Grayson when JT didn't respond. He turned to the woman and said, "I'm sorry, we didn't get your name."

"I'm Nina Walker," the woman stated.

Detective Grayson took out his notepad. "Can you give me your address and phone number?"

"I don't live here. My husband is preaching at a conference tonight," Nina told him, and gave him her address and telephone number in Dayton, Ohio. Nina sat down with the police officer and told him everything she saw. When she was finished speaking with the detective, Nina turned back to JT and asked, "Do you mind if I stay here for a while? I would like to continue praying for your wife and daughter."

"I would appreciate that," JT told her.

Detective Grayson handed his business card to JT. "Give me a call when your wife wakes up, or if you learn anything else that might help us with this investigation."

JT grabbed the officer's arm and said, "You've got to catch this woman. She's destroying my family."

Detective Grayson pulled his arm out of JT's grasp as he told him, "I'll do my best."

A nurse walked out of the ICU and found JT. She told him, "You can go in to see your wife now. She's still unconscious so you can't stay long."

"Okay, I just want to see her," JT told her.

"Do you mind if I come with you?" Bishop asked.

JT could see that Bishop was suffering just as much as he was with everything that had happened. And to top it off, JT knew that he was the cause of everything, so how could he deny this man the opportunity to see his child? "Come with me."

They walked into the small room with a curtain for privacy, and looked at Cassandra as she lay in the hospital bed looking like a sleeping angel. She had bandages on her arm, shoulder, and back. JT's heart broke as tears filled his eyes. This was his wife, and his sins had almost killed her. He walked around the bed and touched the arm that was not bandaged. He intertwined his fingers with hers. Tears were spilling over as he said, "I'm so sorry. I'm so sorry for everything I did to you."

He squeezed her hand tighter and continued speaking through his tears. "If you can hear me, Sanni, and I know you don't want me to call you that anymore, but I love you, Sanni. God knows I have wronged you, but I never stopped loving you." He wiped the drizzle that was flowing from his nose. "I'm a broken and fallen man, but I haven't lost my faith in God this time. I'm trusting that He is going to wake you up." He lifted his face to heaven and said, "Thank you for waking her up, Lord. You know how much I need her."

Bishop stepped closer to the bed. His head was lowered, and his hands formed a steeple underneath his chin as he joined JT in prayer. He said, "Lord, my God and my friend, You know everything about me. You know the good I have done and all the mistakes that I've made. I've only admitted to You and my wife that Cassandra is my daughter. But if you let her live, I promise that I will right that wrong. I will tell the world that this is my daughter and accept all the consequences that come with that."

"Help us, Lord. My wife is the most loving and kind woman I know. She doesn't deserve this. And Lord, please help us to find Lily. Bring her back to us," JT pleaded.

A nurse walked into the room and informed JT and Bishop that they needed to leave.

"When can I see her again?" JT asked, wiping the tears from his face.

"Give her a few hours to rest and then you can come back in."

"Okay," JT said reluctantly as he looked back at his wife. He really didn't want to leave her, but if the nurse was right and rest would help Cassandra recover, he wouldn't be selfish. The knowledge that he was doing the right thing by leaving her room didn't stop his heart from breaking. He lowered his head and kissed her soft lips, something he hadn't been able to do in months. Cassandra hadn't wanted to be this close to him, and he didn't blame her one bit. "I love you, baby. I swear I'll make all this up to you."

He stepped away from his wife, and Bishop took his place. He put Cassandra's hand in his and whispered in her ear. "I'm here, baby girl. I'm so sorry I never told you that I am your father. But I want you to know, I have been proud of you every day of your life. Your father loves you, Cassandra, and I'm going to make this right between us."

JT tapped Bishop on his shoulder and said, "Let's go. The nurse wants us out of here."

They walked back into the waiting room. The woman who had come to Cassandra's aid was still in the waiting room. She was on her knees with her head bowed in prayer. JT appreciated what this woman was doing for his family; he only wished none of this had happened in the first place. He looked at Bishop as a thought struck him, and said, "I forgot to call Mattie."

"God help you," Bishop said.

JT took out his cell phone and dialed Mattie's number. It rang six times before the answering machine picked up. He had no choice but to leave a message. "Mattie, I need you to meet me over at University Hospital. Bishop and I are here because . . . Cassandra has been stabbed." He hung up and put his phone back in his pocket.

He had nowhere to turn. There was nothing he could do for Cassandra or Lily. But looking at this woman on her knees in prayer to God, an idea came to JT. He tapped Nina on the shoulder.

When Nina looked up and saw that JT was trying to get

her attention, she stood up and asked, "Is everything all right with Cassandra?"

"She's still unconscious. I won't be able to see her again for a few hours, so I was wondering if you could take us to the church where your husband is preaching tonight? I'm hoping to get a prayer chain going."

CHAPTER 27

The conference was being held at True Vine, a church JT had competed with for members. But the members of True Vine were sold out for their church in part because of all the mission work the church did. They took members on several mission trips each year to places like Mexico, Africa, and Egypt. True Vine even conducted mission work in their own community—always reaching out and lending a helping hand. JT had respect for Larry Moore, the senior pastor of True Vine, because he had never been caught in any mess. As far as JT knew, Pastor Moore lived a straight-and-narrow type of life and he needed those types of people in his life right now.

JT and Bishop sat on the front pew as Nina went into the pulpit area and whispered into Isaac's ear. As Nina walked back down the stairs toward JT and Bishop, JT watched Isaac say something to Pastor Moore while pointing in his direction.

Pastor Moore came down from the pulpit and walked over to JT. "Can I speak with you in my office?" JT stood up and followed. When the door to Pastor Moore's office was closed, he turned on JT and asked, "What's this all about? Are you trying to make another play for my members?"

JT held up his hands. "Whoa, Larry, I know I've tried to steal a few of your members, but right now I don't even know if I have a congregation to go back to. I'm not here as a pastor, just a man in need of prayer."

Larry put his hand on JT's shoulder. "What happened, man?"

"My wife has been stabbed and my daughter kidnapped by a woman I had an affair with." JT lowered his head. "I've been a fool and I have no right to stand in front of your pulpit. The only thing I can tell you is that when I saw Nina praying at the hospital, I felt that God was directing me to ask your people for help."

"Come with me," Pastor Moore said as he left his office and walked back into the pulpit area. The choir was finishing their last song. Pastor Moore took the mic from the lead singer when she finished, and addressed the congregation. "Praise the Lord, saints. And thank you all for coming out here on a Thursday night to listen to my old friend, Isaac Walker, preach the Gospel." The members of the congregation stood and clapped at the mention of Pastor Walker. Pastor Moore looked at JT and then turned back to his congregation. "Before we hear from Pastor Walker, I need everyone to sit down and listen to Pastor Thomas from Faith Outreach Church." He handed the mic to JT and then sat down.

JT stepped forward and told the crowd, "I'm not going to take up too much of your time. I'm here tonight because I need your prayers. I've seen a lot of you at other events around the city, or you've seen our television program. But you really don't know me." He lowered his head in shame, but he had come this far and was determined to go all the way. "I've been living a life of sin ever since my first child died. I stopped trusting God and now my wife is in the hospital because a woman I had been having an affair with stabbed her."

Collective gasps could be heard through out the congregation. An elderly woman stood up and shouted, "You ought to be ashamed of yourself."

His eyes were watery as his face filled with regret. "Believe me, I am ashamed of what I've done. But I still need your help. My daughter was with my wife when Vivian stabbed her, and—" A knot formed in JT's throat. His shoulders slumped as a river of tears ran down his face.

Pastor Walker stood up and took the mic from JT. He looked out at the congregation and said what JT couldn't. "This woman kidnapped his daughter."

More gasps.

Pastor Walker continued, "Now, I'm sure Pastor Thomas has condemned himself enough, so what he really needs from us right now is our prayers. Right now, I'm asking everyone to get out of your seats and get on your knees. My heart goes out to Pastor Thomas. My wife and son had been gunned down because of something that my son had gotten involved in. But thanks be to God they both survived. So, now I'm asking that we pray that this man's wife will live and that his child is brought back home unharmed."

JT turned to Isaac Walker and said, "Thank you."

"Let's pray," Isaac said.

JT nodded, and got on his knees in the pulpit area along with the other pastors and ministers. When they finished praying, Bishop Turner put his hand on JT's shoulder and pulled him off the floor. He whispered in JT's ear, "Someone wants to speak with you. Come on, let's go."

JT thanked the people for praying for his family, and then followed Bishop out of the church and into the parking lot. His eyes widened as he saw Deacon Benson standing next to his car. "What's going on?" JT asked Bishop.

"Benson thinks he can help," Bishop told him.

JT was skeptical as he approached Benson. When they stood face-to-face, JT asked Benson, "After all I did to you, why would you want to help me?"

"First, I'm not doing anything for you," Benson told him with obvious anger in his voice. "But I like your wife, and as far as I'm concerned, Lily is just as much my daughter as she is yours."

"Benson, I just want you to know that I'm sorry about what I did. I know it wasn't right," JT said.

Deacon Benson said, "I'm not interested in your apology. Just let me tell you what I know so we can go get Lily."

"Fair enough," Bishop responded.

"I'm sure she wouldn't have taken Lily to her house here, because she knows the police would be all over that place. But she has another house on the outskirts of Cleveland. It belonged to her mother, but when she died, Vivian received the house. I know where it is because I repaired her roof and put in a new furnace."

JT took from his pocket the business card Officer Grayson had given him. He called the detective on his cell phone, then handed the phone to Deacon Benson so he could tell him how to find Vivian's mother's house. When they hung up, JT turned to Bishop and said, "I need you to go back to the hospital and sit with Cassandra for me. Mattie will be there by now and you'll need to fill her in on what happened."

"I'll tell her, but you know as well as I do that she is going to go ballistic over the fact that I knew about this before she did," Bishop told JT.

"You were at the house with me when I received the call. So she'll just have to get over that," JT said, then turned back to Deacon Benson. "Let's go."

They rode the highway in complete silence. JT was

grateful that Deacon Benson had set aside his anger in order to help him get Lily back, but he also understood why Benson didn't want conversation. So JT sat on the passenger side and silently prayed to God. He had been spending a lot of time with God lately. He refused to give up or turn away from his Lord this time. No matter how hard things got for him, JT was determined to serve the Lord.

He wanted to sing a praise song, but his heart was too heavy for that. But even though JT wasn't able to praise the Lord for the awful things that had been happening to him, he realized that he did indeed still love God. If nothing else, this adversity had shown him that he didn't have to turn his back on God when times got hard.

Cassandra had loved him and he had destroyed her. When this was all over, JT was going to give some serious thought to the kind of man he wanted to be going forward. But right now he could only pray that God would spare Cassandra's life, and give Lily back to him.

When they turned on to the street where Vivian's other house was, JT noticed several police cars parked in front. "I bet she's in there. Why else would Grayson have all these police officers on her street?" JT said.

"Let's park back here and walk up. I don't think we'll be able to drive to her house; looks like they've got it blocked off," Benson said as he parked the car and they got out.

"Which house is it?" JT asked.

Benson pointed. "She's about five houses up, on the right. It's the white house with green shutters. Do you see the police up there, behind those cars?"

"Yeah, they must be getting ready to bust into it."

They walked up the street, anxious to see if Lily was truly with Vivian at this location. Adrenaline was pumping as they approached the house, but then JT saw the police with guns in hand while they stood in Vivian's yard. Vivian sat on her porch swing with Lily in one arm and a knife in the other.

JT yelled, "No, don't do it, Vivian."

He ran toward Vivian, hoping to get to her before she stabbed Lily, but a police officer tackled him. He fell to the ground as the officer hollered, "Stay down."

Another officer told Benson, "Don't come any closer. We've got a situation here and we don't need any citizens involved."

JT said, "That's my baby. She's got my baby."

The officer stood up and helped JT off the ground. "Sorry about that. Detective Grayson wants us to bring you to him."

"Good," JT said as he followed the officer.

As they walked toward the yard looking for Detective Grayson, the officer said to JT, "This lady is a real whack job. Hopefully you can help us calm her down."

"What's wrong with her?" JT asked. He was stunned by the fact that he hadn't recognized Vivian's crazy side before she flipped out on him.

"I wish I knew. We don't know if she missed her meds, or if she's on some unprescribed meds. But we've got to get this baby away from her, and Grayson thinks you can help."

Grayson was at the bottom step in front of Vivian's porch. His gun was aimed directly at Vivian as he said, "I don't want to shoot you, Vivian. So, put the knife down and hand me that baby."

Vivian's eyes took on a faraway look as she told Grayson, "But this is my baby. I can't give her to you. I can't let anybody hurt her, not like before."

"What happened to your baby before, Vivian?" Grayson asked in a calm, reasonable tone.

"Got to make sure that nothing happens to Jasmine," Vivian said.

JT tapped Detective Grayson on his shoulder. "Thanks for getting here so quickly."

"Who is Jasmine?" Grayson asked without taking his eyes off of Vivian.

"I have no idea," JT said, realizing that he knew next to nothing about this woman. He'd slept with her, but had never bothered to ask any questions, and now his family was being destroyed.

"Put the knife down and give me the baby," Grayson said with a bit more force in his voice.

"Rock-a-bye and good night," Vivian sang to Lily as she rocked her.

"Vivian, please don't do this," JT said. He wanted to go up the stairs and grab his baby, but Grayson held him back.

Vivian looked up and smiled. "JT, what are you doing here?"

"You've got my baby, Vivian. I came to get her back."

Vivian looked at Lily and then turned back to JT. "We didn't have a baby together, JT. You left me before I could get pregnant, remember?"

JT pointed at Lily. "That's my baby, Vivian. You took her from Cassandra earlier today."

Anger filled her eyes as she told JT, "Cassandra tried to steal Jasmine away from me. She tried to steal my baby, but I fixed her."

"Her name is not Jasmine. She is Lily, Vivian. That's my baby."

"This isn't Cassandra's baby. Cassandra has Aaron. This is Jasmine. You're a liar, JT," Vivian said, raising her knife and poking it in JT's direction with every word she said.

Grayson pushed JT away from the steps. "She's getting agitated. We're going to have to try something else."

Benson stepped forward. "Can I try?"

"Who are you?" Grayson asked.

"Lily is my daughter. At least, that's what I thought until a couple of weeks ago," Benson told Grayson.

Grayson waved his hand in the air. "Too much information for me." He told Benson, "Come on, see if you can talk this woman down before I have to do something drastic."

Benson stood at the bottom of the steps. He looked toward Vivian as he said, "I know how it feels to lose a child. It's not a good feeling at all. I thought Lily was mine, but then Diane told me that Lily is JT's child." Tears escaped his sad eyes as he asked, "How did you lose Jasmine?"

"They took her from me; said I wasn't stable enough to keep her." She laughed and then added, "But I got the last laugh on that crazy mother of mine. She gave my baby away, but I got her back."

Tears were still in Benson's eyes, but he played along. "You showed her, didn't you?

"Yep!" Vivian said with the glee of a child on the playground.

"Can I see your baby?" Benson asked.

"You want to see Jasmine?" Vivian asked as she stood up. A look of pride spread across her face as Benson came closer.

As Benson walked up the stairs, JT remembered when Diane had asked him to look at Lily and he had refused. Now, he'd give anything to see Lily alive. *Lord, please don't let her hurt my baby*, JT silently prayed.

"She's beautiful," Benson said as he lovingly gazed at Lily.

Vivian smiled. "She is beautiful isn't she?"

"Can I hold her?" Benson asked

Vivian's smile disappeared as she stepped back and said, "Not you too, Benson?"

"What? What's wrong, Vivian?" Benson asked, his voice elevated with fear.

She continued backing away as she raised her knife. "You're one of them. You want to steal my baby." She was hysterical as she said, "I will kill her before I let you have her."

When Benson had stepped onto the porch, one of the police officers had snuck around the side of the house. As Vivian became hysterical, he jumped over the side of the porch and grabbed the arm that held the knife. Benson then grabbed Lily out of her other arm.

"No. No. Don't take Jasmine from me; not again," Vivian said as the police officer threw her on the ground.

JT fell on his knees, lowered his head, lifted his hands, and gave praise to the Lord. He hadn't praised God on the way there, but he had prayed to Him. JT hadn't turned to God in times of crisis in years. Now, he seemed to always be turning to God, maybe not always in praise, but definitely in prayer. "Lord, You are awesome," JT proclaimed. "Thank You. Thank You so much for sparing Lily's life."

Benson walked off the porch as Grayson put handcuffs on Vivian. He stood in front of JT, and waited for him to stand.

JT rose and wiped his eyes. He was doing a lot of grown-man crying lately and he didn't mind a bit. "Hey, man, thanks for what you did up there. I can't tell you how much I appreciate it."

"I didn't do it for you."

"Yeah, I know. I appreciate it anyway."

Benson handed Lily to JT, and said, "I'm giving her to you for now. But I want to see that DNA test when you get it back."

"I understand. And don't worry, Benson. I won't keep Lily away from you if she turns out to be yours."

Pain was etched across Benson's face as he said,

"Diane says that she knows for sure that Lily belongs to you. So I'm not going to keep her away from you. But if she turns out to be mine, I want her back."

"You're an honorable man, Benson. I wish I were half the man you are."

CHAPTER 28

Detective Grayson gave JT a ride home. He made two bottles for Lily and threw her formula mix in a bag along with wet wipes and a few diapers. As he was rushing back out the door, he remembered that Cassandra always brought an extra outfit for the kids. He ran upstairs and took one of Aaron's old sleepers out of the drawer and threw it in the bag for Lily. He got in his car and raced back to the hospital.

The first person he saw as he entered the hospital waiting area was Mattie. She jumped out of her seat, and JT knew from the fireworks blazing in her eyes that she was getting ready to set it off.

"How dare you come in here!" Mattie screamed at JT.

Bishop had been sitting next to Mattie. JT ignored her and walked over to Bishop. He set the baby carrier on the floor and sat down next to Bishop. "Have you heard anything more from the doctor?" JT asked.

"She hasn't woke up yet," Bishop told him as he looked down at Lily and smiled. "Thank God you were able to get this little one back. I was praying for her."

"Praying for *his* baby? You needed to be praying for Cassandra," Mattie said as she advanced on both men. She turned to JT and said, "Don't try to act like you don't hear me. My daughter is fighting for her life because of you. You are a lowlife and I hope someone stabs you."

JT looked at Mattie with sadness as he told her, "I'm not going to get into this with you right now. I need to check on my wife." He turned back to Bishop and asked, "Would you mind looking after Lily while I go see about Cassandra?"

"No, son, go see about your wife. I'm sure I remember how to take care of a baby," Bishop said.

JT's heart was heavy as he stood up. On one side, Cassandra's dad was calling him son, but on the other, her mother was calling him a lowlife. He wished he knew what God thought of him right now. Had the Lord searched his heart and found him to be a lowlife as Mattie had, or would the Lord, finally, once again call him son?

Mattie ran toward the nurse's station. The woman behind the desk had a startled look on her face as she looked up. "Can I help you?" she asked Mattie.

"Yes. I want you to bar this man from seeing my daughter," Mattie said, pointing to JT.

He had been walking toward the nurse's station so that he could gain access to the ICU. He stopped as Mattie angrily pointed to him as if he were an escaped convict she was turning into the police. He didn't know if he was supposed to run like Harrison Ford in *The Fugitive*, or continue standing there so he could be cuffed and hauled off to prison where he belonged.

The nurse looked at him and then turned back to Mattie and said, "Only immediate family is allowed in ICU, so if he's a boyfriend, he can't come back anyway."

JT continued walking toward the ICU. He told the nurse, "Cassandra is my wife. I need to check on her."

The nurse turned back to Mattie and said, "You can't stop her husband from seeing her."

"Why not? He's the reason she got stabbed in the first place."

The nurse stood up. She put her hand on the telephone on her desk. "Are you telling me that her husband is the person who stabbed her?"

Bishop picked up Lily and rushed over to the nurse's station. "No, ma'am, he certainly did not stab Cassandra."

"How do you know?" Mattie screamed. "You weren't with Cassandra when she was stabbed. You haven't been with her for most of her life if you want to get technical."

Bishop turned to the nurse and said, "A police officer was here with us earlier. The woman who witnessed the incident and called the ambulance also was here earlier. She very clearly described the woman that she saw stabbing Cassandra."

"And the police arrested the woman about an hour ago. The woman had also kidnapped my baby. I just got her back," JT said.

"That's not my daughter's baby. He doesn't deserve to see her. He's no good." Mattie screamed all of these words so loud that others in the waiting area were now either peeking or flat out staring in their direction.

"Mattie, please calm down," JT said.

"Don't you tell me to calm down. You are destroying my child. And you think I'm just going to sit around here and do nothing to stop you?"

"I love Cassandra. Do you actually think I would have ever wanted something like this to happen to her?"

Mattie put her body against the door to the ICU, folded her hands around her chest, and rolled her eyes upward. Her stance was that of complete defiance as she told JT, "You're not going back there."

"Be reasonable, Mattie. You can't stop JT from seeing

Cassandra. As her husband he could stop you from seeing her. But he hasn't done that has he? No," Bishop Turner said.

"Can you call security, please?" JT asked the nurse.

The nurse picked up the telephone and then looked at Mattie. "I really don't want to call security on you while your daughter is in ICU, but if you refuse to remove yourself from that door, I'll have no choice."

Mattie rolled her eyes and kept leaning against the door.

"Stop this, Mattie. If she calls security, they will put you out of this hospital and you won't be able to check on Cassandra," Bishop told her.

Slowly, Mattie moved away from the door. She kept her eyes averted as she walked by JT. She went back into the waiting area and sat down.

"I'm sorry about all that," JT said to the nurse. "Can I go in to see about my wife now?"

She pressed a button to unlock the door to the ICU, then leaned over and whispered to him, "I'm sorry about your wife; *and* your mother-in-law."

"Me too," JT said. He turned to Bishop. "Are you sure you're okay with watching Lily for a little while?"

"You go on in. I've got this little one," Bishop said

However, Lily picked that moment to flex her lung muscle. JT smiled at her. He rubbed her cheek and said, "There, there, little princess. I bet you're hungry, huh?"

"I'll get her bottle out of the diaper bag you brought. Now, go see about your wife," Bishop said.

JT opened the ICU door and walked down the hall toward room number eleven. When he reached the room, he stood there for a moment wishing that he could turn back time. If he could, he would have talked to Cassandra more. He would have told her the truth about how he felt when Sarah died. Maybe if he had done that, he wouldn't have found comfort in the arms of other women, and his wife wouldn't be in the hospital right now.

He shook his head trying to ward off the memories as he pulled back the curtain and walked into Cassandra's ICU room. She was still asleep. He sat down in the chair next to her bed. She still looked so peaceful; like she didn't have a care in the world. He thought about when he had been in a hospital bed a few months ago. Cassandra didn't want to see him, and only visited him twice the entire time he was in the hospital. He couldn't blame her, though. If she had done as much to him as he did to her, he probably wouldn't be sitting there right now.

He wished she would wake up. He had so much to tell her. He grabbed her hand and squeezed it as he told her, "I got Lily back." When he said those words to Cassandra he suddenly remembered something he hadn't paid much attention to earlier. The woman who helped Cassandra told him that when she ran over to his wife, she heard her say, "My baby."

JT smiled, realizing that Cassandra might be thinking of Lily as part hers. With as big a heart as his wife had, JT knew it wouldn't take long for Lily to warm her way into Cassandra's heart. "She's beautiful, isn't she, Cassandra? I'm sorry I did this to our family, but I want to keep her. I hope you decide that you want to stay with me when this is all over, because Lily and I are going to need you. And I think you, Jerome, and Aaron need me also. I'm not the same man that I was, Sanni. Please give me a chance to prove it to you."

As JT sat there staring at his wife, he finally realized how much his sins had harmed his family. With all of the horrendous things JT had done over the past few years, he'd never considered that any of it would hurt his family. Of course he knew that his backsliding had hurt his relationship with God. But he had been mad at God, so JT hadn't cared how he felt at that time. But now that the blinders were off and his eyes were open, he found that he did care.

In truth, he wanted to close his eyes and run away from the realities that had beaten him down. "I'm so sorry, Sanni. I wish I had been a better man." He lowered his head, putting his elbow on his thigh and his hand on his forehead.

The curtain to Cassandra's room was pulled back. Lost in thought, JT jumped when he heard the noise.

"Sorry, I didn't mean to startle you," the doctor said as he walked closer to JT.

"I was just thinking," JT said as he stood up and shook hands with the man.

"I'm Dr. Stevens. We talked earlier, but I don't think I told you my name."

"Yeah, you're right, I don't think I even thought to ask. My mind was so far gone at that time."

"I understand," Dr. Stevens said.

JT turned and looked at Cassandra. "How is she doing? Tell me the truth; will she pull through this?"

"Most of the stab wounds were in her arm and shoulder. So we were able to stitch them up without a problem. However, she had two stab wounds in her back; those are the ones I'm most concerned about. She lost a lot of blood, but I still think she can pull through. We just need to give her a reason to believe in the possibility of pulling through."

"What do you mean?" JT asked.

"I think right now the best thing you can do is to be upbeat and to talk positive around her."

Positive and upbeat? JT didn't know what that felt like anymore. His life had been a tragedy. Everything he touched got all messed up. The only good thing that had ever happened to him was his family, and he had single-handedly destroyed them, too.

CHAPTER 29

So, in order to be positive and upbeat as Dr. Stevens asked him, JT decided to let go of his pity party and remember the good times. He sat back down, put Cassandra's hand in his and drifted back to better days.

Where are you taking me, JT?" Cassandra asked as *they drove down the streets of Cleveland in JT's ten-year-old Oldsmobile.*

"You just sit over there and be patient," JT told her, a sheepish grin on his face.

"You know I'm too nosey to be patient. You've been hiding a secret all week long, and I'm just about going crazy to know what it is."

JT loved how fidgety Cassandra got when she tried to figure something out. She was truly nosey and he loved every minute of making her wait. JT had spent only two Christmases with Cassandra, but each one was enlightening. The first Christmas, he'd purchased her gifts a month in advance. They weren't married yet, so he left her gifts under the tree at Cassandra's house. Every time he would come to visit, he noticed that the presents had been moved from one place to another. Then one day he noticed that a piece of the wrapping had been torn from one of the packages. He'd asked Cassandra, "What happened to the wrapping paper?"

She rolled her eyes and admitted, "I couldn't take it anymore. I pulled off a piece of the paper in order to see what the box said, but the box is blank."

He laughed. "Are you that impatient?"

"I'm terrible. I've never been able to wait until Christmas. Please tell me what my presents are."

From that day on, he tortured her with surprises. He would tell her on Monday that he had a surprise for her, but he couldn't tell her what it was until Friday. Right now, however, he was taking her to see his surprise on Wednesday instead of Friday, because Cassandra had threatened to starve him if he didn't fess up sooner that Friday.

They pulled into the driveway of a small two-story house that was in a low to middle–income neighborhood. "We're here," JT told her as he turned off the engine and got out of the car.

Cassandra got out of the car and asked, "Who lives here?"

"No one right now. It's vacant."

Before Cassandra could ask her next question, Carl, one of the deacons at their church who was also a realtor, pulled up. He jumped out of his car and ran over to them. "Sorry I'm late, Pastor."

"You're fine, Deacon Carl, we just pulled up ourselves," JT said.

"Well, let's go check this place out then," Carl said, rubbing his hands together.

Cassandra pulled on JT's sleeve. "Why are we here, JT? Are we buying this house?"

With a big smile on his face, he said, "You tell me. I

brought you here to see if you like this house as much as I do."

"Okay," she said. "Let's check it out then."

JT and Cassandra walked into the house hand-in-hand. They were currently living in a four hundred square foot, one-bedroom apartment. Space was limited and they were constantly bumping into each other. However, since they were still newlyweds, neither of them minded the close proximity all that much.

Cassandra's eyes got big as she said, "This place has a living room and a family room."

JT ran up the stairs and hollered back down. "Sanni, there are three bedrooms. I can finally have an office to work on my sermons. Come up here and look at the bedrooms."

She did, and she also made note of the fact that there was a downstairs bathroom as well as one upstairs. Once they were finished looking over the house, Cassandra turned to JT and said, "I like it, but can we afford this place?"

They were in a neighborhood where the houses ranged from seventy to ninety thousand dollars. Carl handed Cassandra the flyer with the price of the house on it. "This house is eighty-four thousand dollars. We just got married eight months ago, JT. You're not earning all that much at the church. How can we afford this place?"

"Baby, don't worry about it. I earn enough at the church to pay for this house, and both our cars are paid for."

"My car is six years old and yours is ten. We are going to need new cars within the next few years."

"The church is growing, Cassandra. We will be able to handle this. Come on, honey, trust me with this one. Okay?"

Cassandra looked at the flyer one more time. She

walked through the house again and then turned to JT and said, "Can we really have it?"

"Yeah, baby, we can."

Cassandra handed the flyer back to Carl and told him, "Let's do the contract, but only offer them eighty thousand."

"We used to love that house, didn't we, Sanni? It wasn't much, but we loved deeply in that small house." JT held Cassandra's hand as he continued to reminisce. "We lived in that house when you told me you were pregnant with Sarah. Remember how you ran to the door as soon as I came home and surprised me with the news. That was a good day for us, Sanni." He was about to apologize for the many bad days that came after Sarah died, but then he remembered that Dr. Stevens asked him to remain upbeat.

He tried to think about some good times that he and Cassandra had shared in their current home. But since he was now being honest with himself, he had to admit that there hadn't been many. By the time he'd moved Cassandra into their mini-mansion, JT had already started cheating on her. "What was I thinking?" he asked himself as he pulled his hand away from Cassandra and hit his own head, as if he were in a V-8 commercial.

At this moment, JT couldn't think of anything positive to say, so he stood up and left the room. He didn't want to contaminate Cassandra with his regrets. He went back into the waiting room and told Mattie that she could sit with Cassandra for a while. But before she went in, he said, "The doctor says that we need to speak positively. So, please try to talk to her about good things."

"I'm not a fool. I know what I need to do for my own daughter," Mattie snapped.

"I'm begging you, Mattie, give her a reason to return to us. Don't fill her mind with hate."

She rolled her eyes as she walked through the ICU doors.

JT sat down next to Bishop Turner. He took Lily out of her baby carrier as he said, "I don't know why that woman is so hateful."

Bishop said, "She hasn't forgiven herself for what we did all those years ago. So, she's grown bitter."

"Lord, please don't let me become bitter like that," JT said as he looked down at Lily. She cooed and he said, "Look at you, little one. Why aren't you asleep?"

"She's been a good baby, hardly cried at all," Bishop told JT before changing the subject. "Do you remember when you asked me if I had ever felt forsaken by God?"

Rocking Lily, JT said, "Yeah, the day you put me on suspension."

"I didn't answer your question then, but the truth is, I have felt forsaken." He had a faraway look in his eyes as he continued. "I only strayed from my marriage once and that was with Mattie. I was just trying to comfort her after her husband died. But one thing led to another, and before I knew it, we had Cassandra."

"I know how mistakes are made, Bishop. So, you don't have to tell me," JT said.

"Well, after I made my mistake I felt disconnected from God. It took me two years to get back to where I had been with God. After that ordeal, I never wanted to be separated from my Lord again."

"Yeah, I'm fighting my way back right now. I just wish I knew how long this misery will last."

Bishop looked toward the ICU doors where Mattie had swept through a few minutes before. He said, "That's why I can have compassion for Mattie. I know that she still holds all that guilt. She never figured out how to accept God's free gift of forgiveness. Consequently, she lives a tortured life."

When JT went back into Cassandra's room, he had a whole new view of his mother-in-law. He no longer saw her as his enemy, but rather a victim of sin. JT added Mattie to his prayer list. He decided that he would pray for her until she was free of guilt. He sat down in the chair next to Cassandra's bed and lowered his head to pray.

"Where's Lily?"

JT slowly lifted his head. Cassandra's eyes fluttered as she tried to lift herself up. JT stood up and rushed to Cassandra's bedside. "Don't try to get up, you might pull some of your stitches."

"Where's Lily?" she asked him again.

"She's fine, Cassandra. I got her back and the police put Vivian in jail."

"Thank God," she said, right before she turned away from him and went back to sleep.

JT ran out of the room and alerted the nurse that Cassandra had awakened and spoke to him. The nurse walked into Cassandra's room, and JT ran out to the waiting room to tell Bishop Turner and Mattie the good news.

"She woke up!" JT shouted when he saw them. Bishop was holding Lily, but he and Mattie appeared to be engrossed in conversation.

Bishop halted his conversation mid-sentence and stood up. "Did you say that she woke up?"

JT had run all the way down the hall of the ICU in order to bring the good news to his family. He took a moment to catch his breath and then said, "Yeah, she woke up and asked me about Lily. I told her that Lily was okay and she went back to sleep. Her nurse is in there with her right now."

"I want to see her," Mattie demanded.

"Just let me make sure the nurse is okay with all of us being back there and I'll come back to get everyone," JT said.

"No!" Mattie shouted. "I'm her mother. I'll go back there and see what the nurse has to say. You can sit here and take care of *your* baby." She pulled Lily out of Bishop's arms and handed her to JT. "Change that baby's diaper, while I go see about my daughter."

JT knew that he was well within his rights to stop Mattie from going into the ICU. But he stepped to the side and allowed Mattie to go in, while he held Lily and sat down in the waiting room with Bishop.

Bishop shook his head as he watched Mattie bully her way through the ICU doors. "That woman needs to learn how to forgive."

"Yeah, well, I am holding a baby that I had by another woman. So, I can't really blame her for how hateful she is to me."

Bishop lifted his hands as he said, "I can't throw any stones at you on that issue." Bishop sat down next to JT, and gazed at Lily as she lay peacefully in JT's arms. "Can I give you some advice?"

"Yes, sir. I think I'm going to need some advice right now," JT said as he grinned at Lily.

"Don't choose the church over your family. I don't know if you and Cassandra will be able to stay together after what's happened, but if you do, don't ever look back and don't let the church pull you away from your family."

"I've been thinking about that a lot. I lost my way when Sarah died. I turned to everyone but Cassandra and God. That's how I grew so cold and indifferent." JT shook his head, still trying to get rid of bad memories that just wouldn't go away. "I don't ever want to be like that again."

Bishop put his hand on JT's shoulder. "One more thing, son. Don't hide Lily. Don't make the same mistake I made. My wife and I moved past my mistake, but I never trusted my church enough to tell them the truth, so I was never able to be a true father to Cassandra. I'll have a lifetime full of regret for denying my own child."

"There is still time. For as long as I've know Cassandra, she has worshipped you. Make her proud now, sir."

Bishop leaned back in his seat. He put his hand over his mouth as he appeared to be heavy in thought.

JT laid Lily in her baby carrier and changed her diaper. She kicked her legs out and cried when she felt the coldness of the wet wipe on her skin. JT turned to Bishop and said, "Do you really want to make this up to Cassandra?"

Bishop closed his eyes and a single tear seeped out. He wiped his face and then sat back up. "Of course I would like to make this up to her. She's my daughter and I love her."

"Then be here for her, even when she doesn't want to be bothered with you."

CHAPTER 30

In the morning JT went to the courthouse to attend Vivian's arraignment. He had to make sure that she wouldn't be getting out on bail. JT was thankful when Vivian's attorney announced that the half-million dollar bail was too much for his client. He was now assured that she would not be loose on the streets to terrorize his family anytime soon.

JT ran into McDaniels, the officer who had arrested Jimmy, as he was walking out of the courthouse. "Hey, JT," McDaniels said as the two men shook hands.

"How are things going?" JT asked.

"Things are looking real good. I was going to call you later today to let you know that we're making progress with setting a trial date for Jimmy Littleton. The prosecutor thinks that we will be able to keep Jimmy and put him on trial here before sending him back to New Orleans."

JT shook his head. "Good. The sooner we get this over with the better. But what I don't understand is why he hung around in Cleveland after he ran me over when he could have just moved on to another city."

"My guess is he hoped that you didn't see who ran you over. He had met a woman and moved into her Section 8 apartment by the time we found him. Trust me, he was in no hurry to leave," McDaniels said.

"Well, thanks for everything," JT said as he walked away from McDaniels. He was anxious to get all of this behind him. Not just the thing with Jimmy, but Vivian also. None of it made sense to him. If he lived to be a hundred years old, JT would never figure out why he had been so willing to destroy his life with people like Jimmy and Vivian.

After he left court, JT took the boys and Lily to see Cassandra. She had been transferred from ICU to a regular room that morning. He purchased a two-seater stroller so he could get Aaron and Lily around. When they walked into the room, Cassandra's bed had been elevated so that she could sit up. She was watching *CNN.* "How are you feeling?" he asked her.

Cassandra turned away from the television and smiled as she saw the children. "You brought them."

"I figured you would want to see them today," JT said.

Jerome ran over to his mother and said, "What happened to you, Mommy? Why do you have to be in the hospital?"

She put her hand on her son's head as she tried to think of what to say to him. She knew that the world was filled with violent people, but she also knew that there were a lot of good people in the world. Her son was only three years old, almost four, but she still didn't want to fill his head with the knowledge of good and evil right now. So she simply said, "Mommy got a little banged up, but I'm getting better. I'll be home soon, so don't worry about me."

"You're not going to die?"

"No, Jerome, I'm not going to die. I'm going to be home to fix your oatmeal real soon. Okay?"

"Okay," Jerome said as he sat down and then asked. "Do they have cartoons on this TV?"

"JT, can you change this channel for Jerome?" Cassandra asked.

JT took the remote and found *SpongeBob SquarePants*.

"Right there, Daddy. I want to watch that," Jerome said.

JT turned back to Cassandra and asked again, "How are you feeling?"

"I'm a little sore, but I'll make it," she answered.

"Thank God. I was so scared."

A knock at the door caused Cassandra and JT to turn. The door opened and Cassandra saw a pretty woman with short hair standing in the doorway. She held her breath as she wondered if another one of JT's women had come to assault her. As the woman came further into the room, Cassandra saw that she was holding the hand of a man who was about a full foot taller than her. She looked at the woman's left hand and saw her wedding ring, and breathed again.

"How is the patient doing?"

JT smiled as he shook their hands. "Nina, Isaac, thanks for coming to see about us." He then turned to Cassandra and said, "Do you remember Nina?"

Cassandra was drawing a blank. She shook her head.

"This is the woman who helped you at the mall. She called the ambulance and came out to the hospital with you. She even called me."

Cassandra was filled with gratitude. She turned to Nina and said, "Thank you so much. I don't remember seeing your face, but I thought I heard someone praying for me while I was on the ground. Was that you?"

Nina stepped closer to Cassandra. She extended her

hand and they shook. "My name is Nina Walker and, yes, I did pray for you while we waited for the ambulance." Nina turned toward her husband and said, "This is my husband, Isaac."

Isaac shook Cassandra's hand. He said, "I'm glad you're doing better. Your husband sure was worried."

Cassandra turned to JT with questioning eyes.

He told her, "I went to the church Isaac was preaching at yesterday and asked the members to pray for us." JT turned the stroller around so that Nina and Isaac could see Lily. "I got her back and the police arrested the woman who stole her and hurt Cassandra."

"Praise God. I knew He would come through for you," Isaac said.

JT smiled. "You know something? I also knew He would come through for us. This is the first time in a long while that I didn't doubt my God."

"Well, we're on our way back home; we just wanted to check in on you all before we left town," Nina said.

"You don't live here?" Cassandra asked.

"No, we live in Dayton, Ohio. Isaac was preaching at a revival in your town. I dropped him off to meet with the pastor and went shopping. At the time, I thought I just wanted a new outfit, but now I realize that God sent me to that mall for you and your husband."

"We wanted to know if we could pray with the two of you before we leave," Isaac said.

"I would appreciate that," JT replied.

Isaac and Nina held hands with JT and Cassandra and prayed for their health, happiness, and restoration.

Cassandra and JT thanked them.

Nina and Isaac left the room. JT sat down. He put Cassandra's hand in his and said, "I'm sorry all this happened to you, honey."

She held up her hand, the one that didn't have bandages

on it from stab wounds, and said, "I just want to focus on getting better so I can get out of here and take care of my children."

"That's fine. We can discuss this later. I just wanted you to know how sorry I am." Aaron woke up and started fussing. JT took him out of the stroller and held him. Then the telephone in Cassandra's hospital room rang. JT picked it up and was surprised to hear Elder Unders on the other end of the line. "Hey, Unders, thanks for calling."

"Not a problem. How is Cassandra doing?" Elder Unders asked.

"She's doing much better than yesterday, thank God," JT said.

"I was worried. Thank the Lord she's all right. What about the baby? Were you able to get her back from Vivian?"

"How did you hear about all of this? Did Betty call you?" JT asked.

"Has Betty been out there?" Unders asked.

"She watched the boys for me yesterday. Did she tell you what's been going on with us? Is that how you found out that Cassandra was in the hospital?"

"No, actually a few of our members attended the conference at True Vine and were there when you asked for prayer."

JT was silent.

Unders continued, "I'm not calling to condemn you, Pastor Thomas. I just wanted to let you know that I will be praying for you and your family."

When JT found his voice again, he said, "I appreciate that, Unders. Would you like to speak with Cassandra?"

"Certainly, if you think she's up to talking."

Cassandra had been watching JT while he talked with Elder Unders, and she could tell he was uncomfortable with the elder and possible church members discussing their situation. She took the telephone from JT and smiled warmly as she thanked Elder Unders for calling.

"You know you're one of my favorite people in the world. I was so worried when I heard what had happened," Unders said.

Her smile brightened. "You've always told me that I was your favorite first lady. But now that you are standing in for Pastor, you're not allowed to have favorites."

He chuckled. "I know, I know. Look, Cassandra, my wife and I are praying for you. Please know that if you ever need us, we are here for you."

"Thank you, Elder. I appreciate that," Cassandra said.

After five days of hospitalization, Cassandra was released. JT arrived to pick her up. When Cassandra saw that he was alone, she asked, "Where are the kids?"

"Betty agreed to watch them for me so I could pick you up."

"They haven't released me yet."

"That's okay. We can sit here and talk while we wait for them to release you. I had a couple of things that I wanted to talk with you about anyway," JT said.

"All right, I'm here, so let's get this show on the road," Mattie said as she barged into the room.

"Hey, Mama," Cassandra said with a half-smile.

"Hey yourself. How are you feeling today?" Mattie asked.

"I'm doing better. I'm not as sore," Cassandra said.

"What's he doing here?" Mattie pointed at JT.

"*He* is *her* husband. And I'm here to take my wife home," JT said.

Mattie turned daggered eyes toward Cassandra. "What's he talking about? You haven't changed your mind have you?"

"No. I haven't had a chance to talk to JT yet," Cassandra said.

JT looked from Mattie to Cassandra. "What's going on? What haven't you talked to me about yet?"

Cassandra looked at her husband. If she were being truthful, in the past few months, JT had actually turned into a decent man. One that she could respect, and even love, but too much had happened. The day that Nina and Isaac Walker prayed for them caused Cassandra to think about giving her marriage another try. Cassandra didn't know if her marriage could work, but she did know that she didn't have the strength to work on it. Not right now, anyway. "I'm moving in with my mother," Cassandra told her husband

"What?" JT asked with a shocked expression on his face.

"I know you're not surprised. Not with all that you've done to my daughter. But maybe you are. Men like you think you'll have a doormat forever," Mattie said.

"Mattie, this does not concern you. Please give me a moment to speak with my wife," JT asked his mother-in-law.

Mattie folded her arms and planted her feet.

"Cassandra, can you please ask your mother to step in the hallway so I can speak with you for a moment?" JT asked.

Cassandra looked at her mother. Now that she knew the truth about her father, she wondered if her mother truly hated JT for the things he'd done to her, or if it was self-loathing that caused her to be so evil all the time? "Mother, can you step out into the hall for a few minutes so I can speak with JT?"

"Why do you have to explain anything to him? Did he explain to you why he had a child by another woman?"

"Mother, please. Why do you have to be so mean all the time?" Cassandra said.

"Well, excuse me. I'm just trying to keep you from making a fool of yourself. But if that's what you want, then fine. I'll be waiting in the hall. When you're done listening to his lies, let me know," Mattie said as she walked out of the room.

JT shook his head as his mother-in-law left the room. He turned to Cassandra and asked, "What's going on, honey? Why aren't you coming home with me?"

"I need some time, JT. I just need to think."

JT sat down in the chair next to her bed. His eyes implored her as he said, "I don't want a divorce, Cassandra. Can you promise me that we won't get a divorce?"

She touched his hand as she said, "I always thought that when I got married it would be forever. I thought divorce was the easy way out. But sometimes it seems so hard to stay."

JT tightened his grip on Cassandra's hand. "I know I wronged you, honey. But I swear to you—I'm a different man now. I won't make the same mistakes."

Cassandra's eyes filled with tears that cascaded down her face. JT wiped them away as he said, "Don't cry, baby, just trust me."

"The sad thing about this whole mess is I really do believe that you have changed." She grabbed some tissue, blew her nose, and said, "The change just might have come too late. I honestly don't know if I care anymore."

"Give me a chance, Cassandra. Don't do this to us."

"I need time, JT. I won't file for divorce right away. But I need you to give me some time to decide if I can stay married to you." As she finished her statement, Cassandra saw pain etched in JT's face. Even with all that had happened to them, she couldn't stand to see this man hurt or in pain. She gently touched his face as she said, "You were my love. We had many years that I will remember fondly. So, don't think that I will ever forget that."

"What's going to happen to us, Cassandra?"

"I don't know. But I can't come home with you right now."

"I can't stop loving you just because you want to walk away," JT told her.

Cassandra closed her eyes for a moment. When she reopened them she asked JT, "Where were you when my husband was breaking my heart?"

CHAPTER 31

JT had wanted to talk with Cassandra about some things that had been on his mind when he went to the hospital to pick her up. Instead, he got his heart broken. He was now at home licking his wounds. Cassandra had taken the boys with her to Mattie's house. She'd kissed Lily, and then handed her to JT and said, "I can't take her with me. You'll have to learn how to take care of a baby."

"Can I call you if I have any questions?" he asked with a grin on his face.

"Of course you can," she said, and then she was gone. She'd also taken two suitcases full of clothes with her.

With Cassandra gone, JT noticed just how big the house was. It was lonely with just him and Lily in it. But besides that, JT realized that even if his entire family was in this house, there were still too many rooms for them to use. Since he was still on suspension from his pastoral duties, he roamed around the house aimlessly at times. When Lily was awake, he fed her and changed her diaper. When he had changed about fifty diapers, JT realized that he hadn't changed that many diapers for both his sons put together.

He picked up the telephone and called Cassandra. When she answered, he said, "Is it okay if I call you from time to time?"

"It's okay, JT. What's up?" Cassandra asked.

"I just realized that I wasn't very helpful to you when it came to taking care of our children. I left all the work to you, and I'm feeling pretty bad about that right now."

"I wouldn't feel too bad, JT. You had to work and I stayed at home with the kids. So, of course I would do more with them."

"I guess you're right. It just seems like I'm doing so much more for Lily than I ever did for the boys."

Cassandra laughed. "Well, I can help you out with that. I have a job interview next week, and my mom will be at work, so I need you to keep the boys. Will that be okay?"

"Of course I'll keep them," JT said. He frowned and added, "I thought we agreed that you would stay home with the boys until they were in junior high."

"We're not together right now, JT, but I still have to take care of our sons."

"You don't think I would help you?"

"Be realistic. You've been suspended from the church. You're still getting paid right now. But how long do you think that will last if the church decides to let you go?"

JT hadn't thought about the very real possibility that he would no longer be the pastor of Faith Outreach. What would he do if he was no longer a preacher? How would he take care of his family? A thought crept into JT's mind and he spit it out before he could change his mind. "Do you think we should sell this house? You've always said it was too big for us. We could use the money from the sale to give us a cushion while we see what comes next."

Cassandra hesitated for a moment, but then she said in an awestruck voice, "Are you serious? You would really put that house on the market?"

JT shrugged. "It's just a house. It means nothing to me now that you and the boys are gone."

"What about our old house?"

Cassandra had loved the first house they purchased. JT knew that and still he'd moved her out of it. He never sold the house though. For the last few years they'd allowed church members to rent it. "The Clark's lease is up in about two months. If you want us to move back there, I can let them know that we want our house back."

"Not so fast. I need to think about all of this."

"Fair enough. But are you okay with putting this house on the market so that you can continue to stay home and take care of our boys?"

"Actually, JT, I think that's the best idea you've come up with in a long time."

They hung up and JT walked around the expansive house. He looked into each room and realized that he wouldn't miss the place. He and Cassandra had never really made this house a home, not like they had with their first home. That one they had put so much love into, which was the reason he hadn't sold it.

Lily was lying in the playpen in the family room. JT went back to the family room and checked on her. She was still sleeping, so he spent some time in prayer and then picked up his Bible. He randomly flipped the pages, landing on the thirteenth chapter of Romans. He read:

> *Let every soul be subject unto the higher powers.*
> *For there is no power but of God: the powers that be*
> *are ordained of God.*
> *Whosoever therefore resisteth the power, resisteth*

the ordinance of God: and they that resist shall re-
ceive to themselves damnation.

JT felt as if he understood those verses better now than
he ever had. He had resisted the knowledge of God's
power and it had cost him everything. Now he was no
more than a broken and humbled man. But for some reason, he didn't feel defeated. In all of this, JT had found
hope, faith, and an unshakable trust in God. He had lost
hold of his family, his pastoral position, and he was about
to put his grand house on the market. But he felt like Job
as he looked toward heaven and told God, "Even while
You slay me, I will trust You."

He turned his attention back to the chapter he was
reading and was struck by the eighth verse:

Owe no man any thing, but to love one another:
for he that loveth another hath fulfilled the law.

An image of Jimmy Littleton swept through JT's mind's
eye as he finished reading that verse. He did owe someone. The very man who had been his friend and stood by
him during his time of need, JT had abandoned. JT didn't
necessarily agree with the way in which Jimmy had be-
friended him. Because he had never stolen anything before that day, nor had he thought about stealing after the
events of that night long ago. But he had kept the money,
and he'd used all of it to benefit his own will. Never once
in all these years had he even thought about trying to lo-
cate Jimmy to see how he had fared in life. Nor had he
bothered to pray for his old friend. JT had simply tried to
wipe the memory of Jimmy out of his mind. But he couldn't
do that anymore. He owed a man something, and he was
determined to pay his debt.

* * *

JT's next-door neighbor kept Lily while he went downtown to the jailhouse. Once he showed the guards his clergy badge and asked to speak with Jimmy Littleton, the guards arranged the visit.

Jimmy walked toward the station where JT sat. Once Jimmy realized JT was his visitor, he noticed Jimmy's eyes fill with hatred. JT didn't get upset, he now understood, but he was grateful that the two of them were separated by a glass wall.

Jimmy sat down and picked up the telephone on his side of the room. JT picked up his telephone. Jimmy said, "What are you doing here?"

"I wanted to talk to you," JT told him.

"That's a laugh. You never came to see me any other time that I was locked up. Why would you want to talk to me now?"

"Because I understand why you're so angry with me. I owed you something that you never received from me."

Jimmy harrumphed. "You got that right. You owed me a hundred and twenty-five thou. But you gave my money to Mona so that you could have a better life. Well, what about my life?" Jimmy shouted. "Didn't my life matter?"

JT nodded. "It mattered. I was just too selfish to understand that at the time. But I owe you more than money. I owed you my friendship, and I let you down. Just like I let a lot of people down."

"This is very touching, but I still want my money."

"I understand that," JT said as he raised his hand to quiet Jimmy. "I have already decided to put my house on the market, and if I have to, I will also sell my Bentley. My goals in life right now are to provide for my family and to return what I owe you."

Sarcasm oozed out of Jimmy's mouth as he said, "That's great, maybe I'll buy myself a hundred thousand dollars' worth of cigarettes. Fool, what do you think I can do with that kind of money in here?"

Maybe he was a Johnny-come-lately, but there had to be something he could do to make up for what he hadn't done for Jimmy. A thought came to mind and he asked, "Do you have any relatives who could benefit from the money?"

Jimmy leaned back in his seat. He studied JT for a moment, then asked, "Are you just saying this because I'm locked up and can't do nothing about it if you don't keep your word; or have you had an attack of the conscience?"

"I've had an attack of the conscience big time," JT assured him.

Jimmy sat back up in his seat, his eyes filled with compassion as he said, "There is someone I'd like to do something for. He's nineteen years old and I've only seen him three times."

"Who is he?" JT asked.

"My son. But I've never been a father to him. I never even gave his mother a dime in child support. I'm likely to be in prison for at least twenty-five years. By the time I get out, I'll be ready to collect social security. But you know as well as I do, I haven't worked a day in my life. So, maybe if my son has some money so that he can go to college and make his way in the world, he might take care of me in my old age."

"If you get his address to me, once I've sold my stuff I'll make sure I have a trust set up for him."

"I'll mail his information to you," Jimmy said. He gave JT a stern look before adding, "I'm not joking with you. My boy really needs a hand up in this world. Forget what I said a minute ago. I don't really care if he does anything for me. But with that kind of money, he could go to Princeton or Harvard. Heck, he could even become president of the United States like Obama did."

JT saw the pride on Jimmy's face as he discussed his son's future options. "I won't let you down this time. You can trust me. I'll talk to you soon." JT hung up the phone and stood up. He started walking away.

Jimmy knocked on the window, stopping JT in his tracks. JT came back to the window and picked up the phone. Jimmy said, "My boy's name is Lamont Stevens. That sounds professional, doesn't it?"

"Real professional. He's going to make you proud."

CHAPTER 32

Purging himself of the foolishness of his past was proving to be a cleansing experience; like a baptism. Even with all the trials and tribulations in his life, each day JT woke up and spent time with the Lord. He felt himself drawing nearer to the cross. Although the cross for most people was a place of persecution and pain; for JT it had become a place of peace. This was where he learned to trust God. No matter what the future might bring, JT was sure of one thing: he would serve the Lord for as long as he lived.

"Well, Lily, are you ready to go handle our business?" he asked as he looked down at his little girl. He knew for sure that Lily was his. He'd received the DNA results two days ago and immediately informed Cassandra. She didn't respond to his announcement, just told him that she had to get off the telephone. JT wasn't sorry he told her though. He was tired of hiding, and wanted no more secrets between him and his wife. What did bother JT, however, was the way Benson reacted to the news.

After JT informed him that the DNA test confirmed Lily was his child, Benson's sobs could be heard through the phone. Benson was such a big man that JT never imagined that he would respond in such a way. But heart-wrenching pain has a way of destroying a man. "I'm sorry, Benson. I really am," JT said as he slowly took the phone away from his ear and hung it up.

Lily was in her baby carrier. He picked up the carrier and stepped outside. There was a For Sale sign in his front yard. As he walked to his Bentley, he also saw the For Sale sign in the window of his car. It was another part of his cleansing experience, but JT wasn't finished yet. He was headed to Faith Outreach. He'd made a decision about his future at the church that had given him his first pastoral position, and he was going to discuss his decision with the congregation. He'd told Cassandra what he planned to do last night. He called her every night to keep her informed about the changes going on in his life, and to be honest, he also called to hear her voice. No man knew better than him about the cost of sin. He was paying a heavy price, but he still had blind faith that God was on his side, and would one day lift him up again.

He strapped Lily in the backseat of the car, then got in the frontseat and drove down the street. He turned on his radio and allowed his soul to be soothed by the gospel music streaming through his speakers. "You like this music, Lily? That's Kurt Franklin singing 'Brighter Day.' "

By the time he drove into the church parking lot, Fred Hammond, Mary Mary, and Tonya Baker had all lifted his spirit. He pulled Lily's baby carrier out of the backseat and said, "Let's go, little one."

She looked up at him with her pretty brown eyes and smiled. Then she giggled.

JT stopped walking, as his heart filled with joy. This was the first time Lily had responded to him in such a manner. For a month now, it had been just him and Lily, except for the times when the boys came for a visit. JT could honestly say that he loved all his children and didn't regret Lily. Although, he did regret the circumstances in which she came to be. Life would have been so much easier if Cassandra had birthed Lily. But there was no sense looking back. He had been a willing participant in screwing up his life, and now he was prepared to own up to it. JT hadn't been back to his church since the incident with Cassandra and Vivian. He'd spent his time healing at home, communing with God, and now he was strong enough to come back to the house of God.

As he walked into the sanctuary, JT noticed heads swivel in his direction. Some of the people stared directly at Lily, and then the whispering began. He knew that a lot of his members had heard about Lily being kidnapped. They also knew that Lily was the child he had with Diane. His conversation with Elder Unders confirmed that. The chickens do come home to roost, as his mother-in-law had lovingly told him months ago. But JT was okay with that. He had come to terms with his actions. He'd repented before God. He'd also come clean about everything in his life with Cassandra. She had not forgiven him for everything he'd done to her, but he was hopeful that a change would come on that front, also.

He walked over to the front-row seat Elder Unders had reserved for him, and a smile appeared on his face as he saw Cassandra already seated. He put Lily's carrier on the floor and sat down next to Cassandra. "I didn't know you would be here today," JT said.

"When you told me what you were going to do, I wanted you to be able to look out into the congregation and see a friendly face." She said as she unbuckled Lily and pulled her out of her baby carrier. She began cooing with Lily.

Cassandra had been attending another church with her mother and the boys, but she chose to come to Faith Outreach today for him. This looked a lot like forgiveness to

JT, but since Cassandra hadn't actually said the words, he didn't want to be presumptuous, so he asked, "Have we become friends again?"

In response, Cassandra lifted her pinky finger. She let it curve like a hook. JT then hooked his pinky finger with hers. She said, "Yes, JT, we are friends."

It wasn't a declaration of love, but after everything he'd done to Cassandra, it was more than he'd ever expected. He wiped his face as his eyes filled with water. "That's more than I deserve," he said as he leaned over, hugged Cassandra, and then kissed her on the forehead. "Are the boys in the church nursery?"

"No, they're at our new church with my mother."

Praise and worship began. JT and Cassandra stood with the rest of the congregation and praised the Lord. JT sang, "The name of the Lord is a strong tower, the righteous run into it, and they are saved." He then lifted his hands to the Lord in total surrender. He had come a long way from the man he had once been. He had wrestled with God like Jacob, and had been determined that he would not let go until the Lord blessed his soul. From the outside looking in, many people would think that he still had a long way to go, but JT knew in his heart that he truly was a man blessed by God. If a history book were to be written on his life, it would say that his downfall had actually been the beginning of his uplifting.

Elder Unders and Bishop Turner walked into the sanctuary and into the pulpit area. Cassandra pulled on JT's sleeve and said, "You didn't tell me that he was going to be here."

"I told him what I was going to do and he thought it was a good idea."

As praise and worship ended, and they sat down, Cassandra whispered to JT, "He needs to be the one standing before this congregation confessing his sins. How dare he come here today?"

JT put his arm around Cassandra and pulled her close to him. She was the most forgiving person he knew. She had even decided to befriend him after all he'd done to her. But he understood why she didn't have the same grace for Bishop. She had idolized the man, had wished and dreamed about him being her father. But when she found out that the man she had worshiped for so long was truly her father and he had never said a word about it to her, the dream had been destroyed.

"Give him a chance, Cassandra," JT told her. "He's also in a lot of pain about what he did to you."

Elder Unders stood behind the pulpit. He looked down at JT and Cassandra and smiled at them. JT smiled back. In the past month, he had come to respect Unders. The man took time out from his day once a week to call JT so that they could pray together. If nothing else, JT would be forever grateful for that.

Unders looked out at the congregation and said, "God is good all the time, isn't He, saints?" The congregation responded in kind and Unders continued. "God is good in the winter, spring, summer, and even when we fall, at least that's what my Bible tells me."

Members of the congregation stood up and screamed, "That's right. Amen!" Others said, "Say that, Elder."

Elder Unders quieted down the group, then said, "I have a special treat for you all today. Our pastor is here and he will be speaking to the congregation in just a minute. So, if you truly believe in the grace of God like I do, I want you all to stand to your feet and give God praise for the man of God, Pastor JT Thomas."

Cassandra squeezed his hand as he stood up. JT's legs felt a bit wobbly, but he was determined to finish the journey. He wouldn't punk out now. He took the mic from Unders and then stood behind the podium looking out at the congregation. He used to think of these people as his members. But now he realized that they belonged to God; he had only been assigned to shepherd them. He understood that when he'd first become the pastor of Faith Outreach, but as the years went by, and he'd prayed and sought the will of God a lot less, consequently, the waters got muddied and he'd forgotten his place.

JT opened his Bible and turned to Psalm 51. He read:

> *Have mercy upon me, O God, according to thy loving kindness: according unto the multitude of thy tender mercies, blot out my transgressions.*
>
> *Wash me thoroughly from mine iniquity and cleanse me from my sin. For I acknowledge my transgressions: and my sin is ever before me.*

JT closed his Bible and looked at the congregation. He said, "I have prayed over the words of those verses for many months now, because I have sinned against God, my wife, and against you all. Many of you are aware that I had several affairs on my wife. I now have a child outside of my marriage by a woman who had been a member of this church."

A wave of shock and disbelief soared through the congregation as quick intakes of breaths occurred all around the room. Then an elderly woman in the second row mumbled, "My Lord, my Lord."

JT nodded in agreement with the reaction of the congregation. "I feel the same way myself. I have done despicable things. But believe me, I'm paying for those things now." He looked at Cassandra. She was holding Lily and looking up at him with admiration in her eyes. That was how she used to look at him when they were first married. Until now, he hadn't even realized how much he'd missed that from her. He turned back to the congregation and admitted, "My wife has left me."

All eyes fell on Cassandra, and JT said, "I know that you saw her sitting with me this morning and assumed that she had simply taken me back yet again. But not this time, and I can't tell you how much that hurts." Tears streamed down his face. He pulled his handkerchief out of his pocket and wiped his face. "We have become friends and that's more than I could have ever hoped for. She came here today to support me. Can you imagine that? After all I've done to her, she didn't want me to go through this alone." He looked to heaven, shaking his head, and then he turned back to the people. "I am a man who has been truly blessed by God, I just didn't know it until it was too late. It took being forsaken by the Lord for me to turn my life around.

"I came here today because I don't want you to go through the suffering my family has endured. I don't want you to miss God. As your pastor I realize that I have failed you, and that is why I am formally stepping down from my pastoral position at Faith Outreach."

His members began to cry. JT held up his hand. "No tears, okay? This is not good-bye. I am not leaving God. I am more determined than ever to serve the Lord. I have fallen in love with Him all over again. But now it is time for me to allow God to lead me. I do not want to hinder God's people by being somewhere I'm not supposed to be." He turned to Elder Unders and said, "From this day forward, I don't want you to call Unders 'elder' again. He is now your pastor."

Cassandra sat Lily in her carrier, stood up, and clapped for Pastor Unders. The other members of the congregation followed, as they stood and clapped for the elevation of this Godly man.

When the congregation had quieted down, JT said. "I only ask that you pray for me and my family. We are on a journey toward God and will need all the prayers we can get to stay grounded and rooted in the Lord. I have been cleansed by God and I want to stay that way." JT put the mic down, left the pulpit, and sat back down next to his wife. The congregation stood up once again, and shouted praises to the Lord as they clapped for the cleansing of JT Thomas.

He and Cassandra stayed until the end of the service. Pastor Unders preached a soaring message on forgiveness that touched the hearts of many within the sanctuary. When they were about to leave, Bishop Turner came down from the pulpit, hugged JT, and then turned to Cassandra. "Can I talk to you for a moment?"

Cassandra started to turn away from Bishop, but JT whispered in her ear, "Remember Pastor Unders's message, honey. You've got to forgive."

She turned back to Bishop and asked, "Why weren't you up there confessing your sins today?"

"I guess I'm not as brave as your husband. I'm praying that God helps me in that respect. But it doesn't change the fact that I love you, and have since the day you were born," Bishop said with his hat in his hand.

"Well, I'm hungry, so if we're going to talk, it needs to be over a steak," Cassandra said.

"JT, will you be okay if I steal your wife for the afternoon?" Bishop asked.

JT picked up Lily's baby carrier as he told them, "You two have a lot to talk about. I'll catch up with Cassandra later."

As JT walked out of the church two men followed him out the door. One of them said, "Pastor Thomas, can we speak with you for a moment?"

JT stopped, put Lily's carrier down, and shook hands with the men. "What's up?"

"I'm Lloyd and this is John." He pointed to the man standing next to him. "Anyway, we've been going through a lot of the things you talked about today, so John and I were wondering if we could come to your house to join you for Bible Study?"

"Pastor Unders might not want you guys to have Bible Study with me."

John asked, "If we check with Pastor Unders and he thinks it's okay, are you willing to help us?"

JT didn't respond.

Lloyd said, "Please, Pastor Thomas. We want to be right in the eyes of God. But we need help from someone who knows what it's like to fall from grace. Will you help us?"

JT nodded. "If Unders says it's okay, I would love to have you guys join me for Bible Study."

"Thanks, Pastor, we appreciate it," John told him as the two men walked away.

As JT walked toward his car, the clouds that were in the sky receded and the brightness of the sun beamed down on him. The Lord in all his glorious majesty sat on the throne looking down to earth. The angels gathered around the throne, anxious to see what on earth had caught the attention of the Holy One. A man was walking away from a church building. He was effortlessly carrying a baby, but what caught the angels' attention was the countenance of the man. They didn't see this on humans very often, but when they did, it was usually shouting time in heaven. The man, the angels recognized, had died to his own desires and was now at peace with God.

Pointing toward the man, the Lord smiled and said, "This is my beloved servant, in whom I am well pleased."

The End

Please turn this page for a bonus excerpt from

FORGIVEN

the second book in the

FORSAKEN SERIES

by Vanessa Miller

CHAPTER 1

"What are you doing?" Mattie Davis asked when she walked into her daughter's bedroom and saw her throwing her clothes into a suitcase.

Cassandra Thomas turned to face her mother. With a smile on her face she said, "I'm going home."

Looking heavenward, Mattie proclaimed, "Lord, Jesus, my child has lost her mind again." Mattie sat down on the edge of Cassandra's bed. Her head was bowed low as she shook it from side to side. "Why do you want to ruin your life? I don't understand this at all."

"Stop being so dramatic, Mother. I've been away from JT for six months. It's time I went home."

JT Thomas had once been the pastor of Faith Outreach Church, but once his sins had been exposed, he'd been suspended, and then resigned from his position. JT was now restored back to God, and was an upstanding citizen who went to work at a community center every day and held a weekly Bible Study in his home for men struggling with infidelity. And yes, Cassandra was willing to admit it: she had fallen in love with her husband all over again. So why shouldn't she and her two sons, Jerome and Aaron, go back home where they belonged?

"I suppose this means you're willing to be a mother to that child he had while still married to you," Mattie stated.

"Yes, Mother, I will be just as much Lily's mother as I am Jerome and Aaron's. I've thought long and hard about this, and the way I see it, if another woman was willing to be a mother to me after you and Bishop Turner fooled around and had me, then how can I deny a child my love, just because I didn't give birth to her?"

Mattie's shoulders slumped. "You enjoy throwing that in my face, don't you? Okay, I made a mistake. Your father was a married man. But does that mean you have to pay for my sins for the rest of your life?"

Cassandra sat down next to her mother and put her arm around her shoulder. Her mother was a petite woman of little more than five feet, but she had a loud, boisterous voice that made her seem seven feet tall at times. "I'm not trying to throw anything in your face, but I'm in a predicament and I need your help to get out of it."

"What predicament? What are you talking about?"

"Well, it seems to me that you and Bishop Turner did to Susan what JT and Diane Benson did to me. Susan forgave you and Bishop and found a way to continue loving her husband. All I'm asking for is the chance to do the same thing with my husband."

"But how can you forgive what that man has done to you?" Mattie asked, refusing to see that she had done the same thing to Bishop's wife, Susan.

"The same way that I'm trying to forgive you and Bishop for all the years the two of you lied to me about who my father was. The way I see it, Mother, forgiveness is a choice." Cassandra stood up, zipped her suitcase, and pulled it off the bed. "Thank you for putting up with me and the boys for all these months, but I'm going home, Mother."

* * *

Cassandra put her key in the lock and opened the door. She stood in the entryway and looked around the modest home. It was certainly not the five-bedroom, seven thousand square foot home she shared with JT before moving in with her mother. JT had sold their home after she moved in with her mother. He moved back into the first home they purchased together. It was only thirteen hundred square feet with three bedrooms, but Cassandra had loved everything about this home. Jerome and Aaron ran into the house and started screaming for JT.

When JT walked from the kitchen into the living room, the boys ran to him. He bent down and Jerome and Aaron jumped on him. "Daddy, Daddy, guess what?" Jerome said.

Laughing, JT said, "I can't guess, so please hurry up and tell me."

"We're home for good!" Jerome shouted.

"You are?" JT asked playfully.

"Yes, Mom said so." Jerome turned to Cassandra and asked, "Isn't that right, Mom? No more sleeping at Granny's house during the week and here on the weekends. We get to be here with Daddy all the time now, don't we?"

The excitement in her son's voice brought tears to Cassandra's eyes. How she wished that she had never moved him away from his father, but at the time, she had no idea that she would ever come home again. So she and JT had agreed on shared custody. Just as Jerome had said, she had the boys during the week and JT had them on the weekend. "Yes, honey, we are home for good."

JT smiled as he stood and walked over to Cassandra. "I made dinner."

"You did not," Cassandra said as she put down her suitcase and walked into the kitchen. Not once in the nine years she and JT had been married had he ever volunteered to fix dinner. He expected his meals to be on the table the minute he was ready to eat, but he didn't bother to help with anything remotely related to kitchen duties.

As Cassandra lifted the lid on the skillet, JT said, "It's just Hamburger Helper."

"No," Cassandra said as she grinned from ear to ear, "what we have here is a miracle."

"Do you think the boys are ready to eat?" JT asked Cassandra.

"They haven't had anything since lunch, so I'm sure they're ready. What about Lily, is she sleeping?"

"Yeah. I put her down for a nap a while ago though, so I better go check on her."

Cassandra put her hand on JT's arm as she said, "No, let me go check on her."

"Okay, well if you're going to get Lily, I'll help the boys wash their hands."

"Mr. Helpful, huh? Be careful, JT, I just might get used to this," Cassandra told him as she headed upstairs.

Lily was sitting up in her baby bed. Her big brown eyes were filling with tears as she opened her mouth to proclaim that she was awake, and didn't appreciate being left alone. Cassandra took her out of the baby bed and held her close as she rocked the screaming child.

"There, there, Lily, it's not that bad." Cassandra sat down in the chair next to Lily's bed, and continued to hold the child until her sobs subsided. She saw JT's features in Lily, just as she saw them in Jerome and Aaron. Funny thing was, looking at Lily and knowing that JT was her father didn't bother Cassandra anymore. Now she knew for sure that she was ready to be a mother to Lily. She began to sing to her, "There's a Lily in the valley and you're bright as the morning star."

JT hollered up the stairs, "The boys are starving, are you two coming down so we can eat?"

"Sounds like your daddy is starving and trying to blame

it on the boys." Cassandra bounced Lily on her lap and then said, "Come on, honey, let's go eat,"

JT was standing at the bottom of the stairs waiting on them. "What were you two doing up there?"

Cassandra rubbed JT's stomach as she put her feet on the bottom step. "Sorry, I forgot how hungry you get."

"I'm a growing man. I need to eat on the regular."

The boys were seated at the octagon-shaped table that was only big enough for four chairs. Cassandra placed Lily in her high chair and then told JT, "We need to pick up Aaron's high chair from my mother's house in the morning. He really isn't big enough to sit at the table." Only six months had passed since she last lived with JT, so the children hadn't grown all that much. Jerome was now four years old, Aaron was eighteen months, and Lily was ten months.

"Yeah, he does look a little awkward in that chair," JT said as he watched his son's legs dangle in the air. They were about two feet away from the ground, so there was no way that Aaron would be able to get out of that chair without help. JT put a plate of Hamburger Helper in front of each child.

"You help Aaron and I'll feed Lily," Cassandra told JT.

Dinner was a big hit. The boys absolutely loved it. Lily's noodles and hamburger pieces had to be chopped up, but she loved the meal as well. After dinner, the family watched TV in the family room until bath time. Cassandra was bathing Aaron and Lily when JT walked into the bathroom with her suitcase.

"This was still by the front door. Does it have the boys' stuff in it or yours?"

Cassandra pulled Lily out of the tub and started drying her off. "Some of my clothes are in that suitcase. I knew the boys had clothes here, so I figured we could go pack up their stuff together."

"That's fine. I'll just put your suitcase in our bedroom."

Alarm registered on Cassandra's face. She lifted her hand to halt JT. "Let me finish up with the kids before we make any decisions."

With a raised eyebrow, JT said, "What decisions?"

She finished drying Lily, handed her to JT, then took Aaron out of the tub and dried him off. "Let's put them to bed and then we can talk."

They put on the kids' pajamas then laid them in their beds. Jerome had already bathed and was sound asleep. JT grabbed Cassandra's hand and pulled her out of Jerome and Aaron's room. "Let's talk."

They walked into their bedroom. Cassandra saw her suitcase in the corner and froze. JT gently pulled her the rest of the way into the room. "What's wrong?" JT asked.

"Nothings wrong, I just thought that we might want to wait a little while before I moved back into our bedroom."

"Where are you going to sleep, Cassandra? We only have three bedrooms in this house and they're all taken."

Wringing her hands and looking everywhere but at JT, Cassandra said, "I thought I would sleep in the room with Lily for a little while."

JT sighed as he let go of Cassandra's hand and sat down. He looked at his wife and he said, "That's not going to work for me, Sanni."

There had been a time when Cassandra had asked JT not to refer to her as Sanni anymore. That nickname meant a lot to Cassandra. It made her feel special and like she really mattered to JT. When he had done all his dirt, she no longer felt special to him, but times were different now.

"I don't plan to sleep in Lily's room forever. I just want to make sure this is going to work between us," Cassandra reasoned.

JT shook his head as he stood up and walked toward

Cassandra. He put her hand in his. "I want a real marriage, and that includes you sleeping in here with me."

"But . . . but what if something happens? What if we can't make a go of this?" Cassandra asked with fear in her eyes.

"I know I let you down before, Sanni, but I'm a different man now. I will never hurt you like I did before."

What had Cassandra said to her mother earlier? Something about forgiveness being a choice? Maybe trust was a choice, also. Maybe she just needed to throw caution to the wind and just lean in. She wanted to forget about the past and move forward with JT as if nothing had ever gone wrong in their relationship.

When she didn't answer, JT said, "Have a little faith, baby. We are going to make this work."

Mattie was screaming inside Cassandra's head, telling her to look before leaping, but she denied the voices in her head and went with the feeling in her heart. "Okay, JT," she said. "We will have a real marriage." Cassandra then closed her eyes and allowed herself to be swept into JT's arms. She loved this man and wanted to spend the rest of her life making love to him. As they came together in love, Cassandra silently prayed, *Please, God, if this is a dream, don't let me wake up.*

Reader's Discussion Question

1. At the beginning of *Forsaken* the reader discovers that Pastor JT Thomas is living a life of sin. Several of his members are also living in sin. If you attended a church where the pastor was openly sinning, would you stay? Would you fall into sin also?

2. Do you believe that a pastor is held to a higher degree of morality than the members of the congregation? If so, why?

3. JT turned his back on God after his first child died. Has there ever been a situation in your life that made you want to give back your membership card to Jesus?

4. Most people have fallen into sin at one time or another in their lives. But do you know that through God's precious son, Jesus, we can be forgiven?

   - Acts 5:30–31
   - Ephesians 1:7
   - Colossians 1:14
   - 1 John 1:9

5. Because of JT's actions, Cassandra no longer trusted him and their life together became unbearable. Even as JT began to change, Cassandra became angry about JT's ability to reach out to God. Do you think she was

too hard on him once he began to change, or do you think she wasn't hard enough on him?

6. JT's mother-in-law, Mattie Daniels, did not trust preachers at all, but she had secrets of her own. If you were counseling Mattie, what would you say in order to get her to understand that not all preachers are sinful?

7. Although Bishop Turner took care of Cassandra and was there for her when she needed him, he wasn't honest with her or the members in his fellowship. Bishop never came clean about the affair he had had with Mattie. If that was the only time Bishop Turner had fallen into sin, do you think it was necessary for him to confess this sin to the members of his fellowship? Why or why not?

8. JT could not control the actions of the other women in his life. Margie Milner called his house to inform Cassandra about her affair with JT. Diane Benson got pregnant and dropped the baby off on JT's doorstep. Finally, Vivian Sampson lost her mind and attacked JT's wife. Knowing what you know about how adultery can affect your family, do you think it is worth it? Why do you think people do it anyway?

9. God requires faith in believers. However, JT thought he had good reason for his lack of faith. What do you think? Is there ever a time when God excuses our lack of faith?

- Deut 32:20
- Matt 6:30
- Mark 4:40

- 1 Tim 5:8
- Psalm 12:1–3
- Matt 24:48–51
- Luke 16:10–13

10. Faith is an important aspect of the believer's life. Meditate on the following scriptures to see what the Bible says about being counted faithful.

- Neh 13:13
- Psalm 101:6–7
- Prov 14:5
- Prov 20:6–7
- Matt 24:45–47
- Matt 25:21
- I Tim 3:1–7
- Heb 3:5
- Rev 2:10

About the Author

Vanessa Miller of Dayton, Ohio is an Essence best-selling author, playwright, and motivational speaker. Her stage productions include: **Get You Some Business, Don't Turn Your Back on God, Can't You Hear Them Crying** and **Abundant Rain**. Vanessa is currently in the process of turning all the novels in the Rain Series into stage productions.

Vanessa has been writing since she was a young child. When she wasn't writing poetry, short stories, stage plays and novels, reading consumed her free time. However, it wasn't until she committed her life to the Lord in 1994 that she realized all gifts and anointings come from God. She then set out to write redemption stories that glorified God.

To date, Vanessa has written the Rain Series and the Storm Series. The books in the Rain Series are: **Former Rain, Abundant Rain,** and **Latter Rain**. The books in the Storm Series are: **Rain Storm** and **Through The Storm**. These books have received rave reviews, winning Best Christian Fiction Awards and topping numerous Bestseller's lists. Vanessa believes that each book in The Rain and Storm Series will touch readers across the country in a special way. It is, after all, her God-given destiny to write and produce plays and novels that bring deliverance to God's people.

Vanessa self-published her first three books, then in 2006 she signed a five-book deal with Urban Christian/Kensington.

Her books can now be found in Wal-Mart, most all major bookstores, including African American bookstores and online bookstores such as Amazon.com.

Vanessa is a dedicated Christian and devoted mother. She graduated from Capital University with a degree in Organizational Communication. In 2007 Vanessa was ordained by her church as an exhorter, which of course, Vanessa believes was the right position for her because God has called her to exhort readers and to help them rediscover their place with the Lord.

A perfect day for Vanessa is one that affords her the time to curl up with a good book. She is currently working on a new novel outside of the Rain and Storm series. She is also preparing the stage production for the **Former Rain** novel. Go to: *www.vanessamiller.com* for more info on Vanessa and her books.

Urban Christian His Glory Book Club!

Established January 2007, *UC His Glory Book Club* is another way by which to introduce to the literary world, Urban Book's much-anticipated new imprint, **Urban Christian** and its authors. We are an online book club supporting Urban Christian authors by purchasing, reading and providing written reviews of the authors' books that are read. *UC His Glory* welcomes both men and women of the literary world who have a passion for reading Christian based fiction.

UC His Glory is the brainchild of Joylynn Jossel, Author and Executive Editor of Urban Christian and Kendra Norman-Bellamy, Copy Editor for Urban Christian. The book club will provide support, positive feedback, encouragement and a forum whereby members can openly discuss and review the literary works of Urban Christian authors. In the future, we anticipate broadening our spectrum of services to include: online author chats, author spotlights, interviews with your favorite Urban Christian author(s), special online groups for *UC His Glory Book Club* members, ability to post reviews on the website and amazon.com, membership ID cards, *UC His Glory* Yahoo Group and much more.

Even though there will be no membership fees attached to becoming a member of *UC His Glory Book Club*, we do expect our members to be active, committed and to follow the guidelines of the Book Club.

UC His Glory members pledge to:

- Follow the guidelines of *UC His Glory Book Club*.
- Provide input, opinions, and reviews that build up, rather than tear down.

- Commit to purchasing, reading and discussing featured book(s) of the month.
- Agree not to miss more than three consecutive online monthly meetings.
- Respect the Christian beliefs of *UC His Glory Book Club*.
- Believe that Jesus is the Christ, Son of the Living God

We look forward to the online fellowship.

Many Blessings to You!

Shelia E Lipsey
President
UC His Glory Book Club

**Visit the official Urban Christian Book Club website at *www.uchisglorybookclub.net*